"You'd be hard to forget," he said in a voice gone low and husky.

"Probably for all the wrong reasons," she returned. His proximity had stolen her ability to breathe and started her pulse thrumming.

His hand slid upward, tracing a line along her skin from the hollow of her throat to her nape, threading into her hair. "Never cared much for saints." Bending to her, he brushed his mouth against hers, the bare touch sending a tremble of longing through her. "I don't think you do, either. Maybe you should stop trying to be one."

Obviously he had never tried, because the way he tempted her, how he made her feel—made her *want*—was sin personified. Not bothering to put up a show of resistance that both of them knew would be a lie, she tugged him to her, turning the tables on him by kissing him.

Dear Reader,

It's with some remorse we write this letter to you about the last book in our THE BROTHERS OF RANCHO PINTADA series. We didn't expect that the most recent place we've been to, the small fictional town of Luna Hermosa in northern New Mexico, would become so much a part of our thoughts and daily lives. However, the time has come for us to visit new places and new characters we hope to share with you.

We developed the series initially wanting to write an evolving family story about people with imperfect lives finding perfect love. Luna Hermosa quickly came to life for us with a colorful community of families and friends who grew closer to each other with each successive story, and dearer to our hearts with each book.

So it's with satisfaction and a twinge of sorrow we say goodbye to Ry, Risa and all of the other wonderful citizens of Luna Hermosa. But who knows, maybe someday their children will come back and tell us their stories as well....

Nicole Foster

SEVENTH BRIDE, SEVENTH BROTHER

NICOLE FOSTER

D1649371

SPECIAL EDITION®

Published by Silhouette Books

America's Publisher of Contemporary Romance

SILHOUETTE BOOKS

ISBN-13: 978-0-373-65473-4

Recycling programs
for this product may
not exist in your area.

SEVENTH BRIDE, SEVENTH BROTHER

Books by Nicole Foster

Silhouette Special Edition

*Sawyer's Special Delivery #1703
*The Rancher's Second Chance #1841
*What Makes a Family? #1853
*The Cowboy's Lady #1913
*The Bridesmaid's Turn #1926
*Healing the M.D.'s Heart #1966
*Seventh Bride, Seventh Brother #1991

Harlequin Historical

Jake's Angel #522
Cimarron Rose #560
Hallie's Hero #642

*The Brothers of Rancho Pintada

NICOLE FOSTER

is the pseudonym for the writing team of Danette Fertig-Thompson and Annette Chartier-Warren. Both journalists, they met while working on the same newspaper, and started writing historical romance together after discovering a shared love of the Old West and happy endings. Their twenty-year friendship has endured writer's block, numerous caffeine-and-chocolate deadlines, and the joyous chaos of marriage and raising five children between them. They love to hear from readers. Send a SASE for a bookmark to PMB 228, 8816 Manchester Rd., Brentwood, MO 63144.

To the B. brothers,
who together know just about everything about skiing,
rafting, mountaineering and cycling as well as knowing
how to love life and find adventures everywhere.

Chapter One

There's no place like home.

It was stuck in her head like a taunt.

Home was the last place Risa Charez wanted to be.

She'd been back in Luna Hermosa, New Mexico, for less than a week and was already convinced it was a mistake. It should have been a joyous homecoming after more than a decade, a return to the town of her childhood and all the memories of growing up in a place she loved.

Except it didn't feel like home anymore. The reunion had been awkward at best, and the memories, the ones as jagged and sharp as if they'd been made yesterday, had reopened wounds that had never really healed.

She leaned her head against the window frame of the tiny bedroom at the back of her father's house and stared at the pasture and the mountains beyond, painted in the warm colors of autumn with the contrast of a brilliant turquoise sky. This had been her room once, a lifetime ago, this vista a beloved view. She could recount every time she'd been here in the last eleven years, for they'd been few: her mother's death, the obligatory Christmases, her eighteenth birthday and the last time she could lay claim to this room as her own.

But she had never come back for more than a few days. Until now.

A light tap on the door drew her away from her memories, and she went to open it, knowing it would be her father.

"We're getting ready to leave." Joseph Charez studied his youngest daughter for a moment, his dark eyes filled with questions Risa knew he wouldn't ask. "Are you sure you won't change your mind and drive over with us?"

"No, thanks. I've got a few things I want to finish up here first," Risa told him. She fiddled with the silver ring she wore, an unconscious reflex in response to her second—third, fourth—thoughts about promising her father and her sister, Aria, she'd meet them at Rancho Pintada. "You go ahead. I won't be far behind."

Aria had insisted she be included in the party at Jed Garrett's sprawling spread held in advance of the official ceremony to toast the success of Aria's latest venture, the opening of a ranch for children with special needs.

Aria had spearheaded the project, and after years of planning and hard work, It was finally coming to fruition.

That Aria wanted her there as well surprised her. It had been almost a year since she'd last seen her sister, and that had been during one of those quick holiday visits, at their father's house, talking but never really saying anything important to each other. Since then,

Aria had married one of the Garrett sons, had a baby and, in the completion of the children's ranch, seen her lifelong dream become reality.

The town's celebration of her sister's accomplishments revived all Risa's old insecurities. She had come home alone, tired of running to escape her past, only to find Luna Hermosa never forgot and that she was still the daughter who'd broken her parents' hearts. She might have been sixteen again, facing the worst time of her life. Everything and everyone was a reminder of how she'd spent the last thirteen years trying and failing to find redemption for her sins.

"You don't have to do this alone, Risa," her father said quietly.

"Do what? Go to Aria's party?" Risa forced a laugh. "I'm pretty sure I can find my way to Rancho Pintada by myself."

Joseph slowly shook his head. He suddenly seemed older, as if her arrival had added more gray, deepened the lines on his forehead, and drained a little of the energy out of his tall, wiry frame.

He lightly touched her face, and the mixed compassion and uncertainty in his searching look made her glance away. "I never understood why you ran away from us. You were just a child, barely sixteen. That whole year you were gone, we never heard from you. And when you came back you'd changed so much, and then it was only months and you were gone again. I don't know what happened to you, Risa. You wouldn't tell us anything. But I know whatever it was hurt you."

"Dad, please. That was a long time ago. It's over with now." She turned away from him because face-to-face he would know she lied. "I'm fine."

"No, it's not over. It's still hurting you. It's why even though you've come home, I still don't have my daughter back."

Her throat tightened painfully, and she swallowed hard against it, fighting tears. "I can't ever be what you want. I never could be. I'm not Aria." She hated herself for saying it as soon as the words left her mouth. All she'd done was to expose petty jealousies and insecurities that she'd have done better to bury and pretend were long dead. "I'm sorry," she said hurriedly before her father could respond.

"Don't be," he said. "It's the truth." When she jerked back at his bluntness, he smiled a little. "You're right. You aren't Aria. But I never wanted you to be. I'm sorry you ever believed differently."

He hugged her, sparing her the need to answer, and she briefly clung to him, wanting in that moment to be again the little girl who depended on her daddy to fix her hurts and shelter her from life's storms.

An hour later, on her way out of town, she reflected it had been a long time since she'd felt like that: secure, at peace with herself and sure of her place in her family's hearts.

An insidious little voice of temptation told her she didn't have to do this, didn't have to put herself on display at a very public event and invite people to look and whisper and speculate on the return of the prodigal daughter. She could easily turn around, call Aria's cell and make some excuse as to why she couldn't make it.

She almost did it. Her foot readied to hit the brake; her hands twitched to turn herself around.

Then she saw the burning car.

* * *

Ry Kincaid hefted a shovelful of dirt on the engine fire, soundly cursing the decrepit Land Rover Discovery, its rotten timing in dying in the middle-of-hell nowhere and his own stupid impulse to come to New Mexico in the first place.

The large black bull mastiff dog patiently sitting a few feet away stared dolefully at him as if confirming Ry's opinion of the situation. He scowled at it, and the dog gazed back, unperturbed.

"Next time I take a call from Duran Forrester," he grumbled at it, "bite me."

Right now, Forrester was first on his list of people he'd be happier not knowing existed. If it hadn't been for him, Ry wouldn't be here, would still be the man with no roots, no commitments, no one tying him to a place or responsibilities.

Instead, Forrester had turned him into something else: a twin brother, with a father and five other brothers and innumerable other relations he hadn't bothered to remember.

Ry'd known nothing about his past, except that he'd been abandoned at birth. Then Forrester had tracked him down, claiming to be his twin and looking for someone to save his son, Noah. Noah had needed a bone-marrow transplant, but Ry hadn't been a donor match. Only one thing had come out of the potential donor testing: the proof he and Forrester were brothers.

In the months since, Forrester had been persistent in encouraging Ry to come to Luna Hermosa and meet with Jed Garrett, the man who'd fathered them, and his other newly acquired relatives. Ry wasn't sure he wanted the reunion.

The hardened side of him, too long alone, wanted to

ignore their existence and go back to the solitary life he was comfortable with. But there was a small, vulnerable part of him that kept insisting this could be his only chance to have a taste of the family life he was denied growing up. That part made him angry—because he was powerless to deny it.

He forcefully jammed the blade of the shovel into the ground as an alternative to using it to beat the hell out of the Land Rover. He needed to deal with the immediate problem instead of screwing around trying to figure out what he was going to do about people he'd never met.

Stuck a good ten miles from his destination, with a vehicle that could charitably be called a scrap heap and a cell phone he hadn't bothered to recharge in several days, he was weighing his options when a car came into view. Slowing and pulling to a stop alongside him, the driver cranked down the passenger-side window and leaned over toward him.

"Do you need some help?"

If it had been a man asking, he wouldn't have hesitated. But it was very definitely a woman. He only had a partial picture of her, stretched as she was over the seat: a slender arm concealed by a long-sleeved black shirt; chin-length hair the color of dark caramel that slanted over one cheek and threatened to get in her eyes, framing features more sensually attractive than classically beautiful.

Her expression held a hint of wariness as she took in Ry, the dog and the still-smoking Land Rover. "I can call someone for you," she offered. "Where were you headed?"

"Rancho Pintada," he said shortly. He kept his distance, though, and began petting his dog, who had lumbered over to his side.

"Have you met Jed, yet?" Risa asked him. "I guess you know he's in the hospital."

Ry gave a curt nod. "That's why I'm here. I figure with him being sick, it's now or never."

The fall that had put Garrett into the hospital had been the deciding factor in Ry's trip to Luna Hermosa. Duran had told him the man already had cancer; he'd broken his hip in the fall and then come down with some sort of infection. From what he'd gathered, the family worried that Garrett might not be able to overcome the combination. If Ry wanted to meet the man who'd fathered him, his brother emphasized now might be his only chance.

"I got into town yesterday, but haven't seen him yet," he said. "Seems like a funny time to have a party."

"The opening ceremony was planned weeks ago. Besides, my sister, Aria, said Jed insisted everyone go ahead because—" she slipped into an imitation of a graveled male voice "—he hadn't planned on goin' to another damned party just so he could listen to all the old hens in town talk about what a bastard he was."

"I like him already."

"You'd be one of the only ones," Risa said with a laugh. "So, do you still want that ride? I'm already late, and if I drive really slowly we can probably miss most of it."

My kind of woman, he thought, at the same time wondering at her reluctance to join the gathering. "You sure?"

"About the driving slowly or the ride?" she asked, then shook her head, indicating she didn't need a reply. "Yes to both. The three of us will be a tight fit, though. I'm not going to have room for—" she glanced behind him to the Land Rover "—for much of whatever it is you've got piled up in the back of that thing."

"Room and board," he said briefly. "And I'll settle for Bear and me. I'll come back for the rest of it later."

She walked around to open the trunk of her car while he jerked the shovel out of the dirt, tossed it in the back of the Land Rover and retrieved his hat, duster and backpack. He slammed the hood and locked the doors.

The difference in their heights was even more pronounced as he brushed by her to stow his things in her trunk. The top of her head would barely graze his shoulder, yet for a small woman on the thin side of slim—Bear far outweighed her—she had generous curves, hugged by her shirt and the forest-green jeans she wore. He caught himself looking, stopped, and forced himself to focus on how the three of them were going to manage in her small excuse for a car.

Turning to her to make a suggestion, he froze.

She was offering her hand to Bear in a slow, deliberate motion, her eyes locked on the dog's all the while. Ry started to protest, but held it as Bear seemed to give her due consideration, sniffing at her hand before lightly pushing at her palm with his nose.

Risa smiled and scruffed him behind the ears. "You're not as tough as you look."

Apparently not, Ry silently agreed. Bear's acceptance of her caught him off guard; his dog rarely warmed to anyone, and then only reluctantly.

"I thought we'd better make friends if we're going to be traveling companions," she said, the smile shifting toward him.

"Does that go for us, too?"

Cocking a brow, her dark eyes swept him up and down. Then, as if she'd decided something in his favor, she held out her hand. He took it in a handshake, engulfing her fingers in his, rough sliding against soft, gripping for a moment extra before slipping his hand away.

"Allies, at least," she said. She started toward the driver's side, leaving him to coax Bear into the backseat.

"Allies?"

"Besides Jed, we're probably the only ones in town who'd rather avoid all the festivities."

Ry shoved the passenger seat as far back as it would go before folding himself into the narrow space. Bear stuck his head between the two of them as Risa slid in beside him.

"Sorry. This car wasn't meant for big dogs or anyone taller than an average twelve-year-old."

"I've noticed," he muttered. As they started in the direction of Rancho Pintada, to distract himself from the uncomfortable ride, he returned to her comment that had spiked his curiosity. "Being the bastard son and the stranger in town gives me an excuse for avoiding the festivities. What's yours?"

Her gaze momentarily slid sideways before she firmly fixed it back on the road. "Half of Jed's sons can claim the bastard title. And I'm nearly as much a stranger as you are. If you don't count the two or three days a year I'm here and gone, it's been thirteen, almost fourteen years since I could call this place home."

She hadn't really answered the question, and it wasn't his business anyway. He understood reticence in parting with anything personal, whether information or feelings; he'd spent a lifetime cultivating the habit. So he kept quiet, instinct warning him that she wouldn't appreciate either his curiosity or his insights. Neither of them said anything else during the short drive. The only sound in the car was Bear's panting breath and the dog's shuffling around in an attempt to find a comfortable position on the narrow backseat.

Fifteen minutes later, she was slowing on the approach to a massive arched wrought-iron and pine gateway when her cell phone went off, the tones unnaturally loud in the small space.

Fishing it out of the driver's door pocket, she glanced at the number and muttered, "Oh, damn, I knew it." She threw him an apologetic look and punched the talk button as she pulled to a stop by the gates.

"Aria, I—I know, I'm sorry." She glanced to Ry again. "I got held up. I'll explain later." There was a pause, then: "No, I'm fine. Yes... Okay, I'll meet you there." Her pained wince said her sister wasn't ready to believe that claim. "Something happened and I... Look, I'm at the gates now. I'll be there, I promise."

She clicked the phone closed and shoved it back in the side pocket, blowing out a long breath. A muscle twitched along the delicate line of her jaw as she stared in front of them.

"My guess is we're a little late," Ry ventured. At her nod, he reached around to ruffle Bear's head where it bumped his shoulder. "So how far is this place you're supposed to be at?"

Her expression thanked him for not questioning the call and what was obviously an uncomfortable situation.

"Not far. It's on your brother Josh's property, more or less next door." She chewed at her lip, twisting the silver ring she wore, then said, "I have to go. It's a family thing."

"Whatever." She might have well have said it was a Zimbabwe tribal thing for all he knew about *family*.

"You don't have to come with me, though."

"You kicking us out?"

"If that was my plan, I would have let you walk to begin with. I'll drive us over there, and then you can take my car and go back to Rancho Pintada or wherever it is you're staying. I can get a ride with my dad and catch up with you later."

"You're pretty trusting of someone you just met."

"The worst that can happen is I lose my luxury car. Besides—" she smiled into his eyes, this time a genuine full curve of her mouth that momentarily threw him off balance and distracted him from what she was offering "—I like Bear. *He* shouldn't have to walk."

Bear whuffled his agreement, allowing her to rub his head. At the same time, he eyed Ry as if challenging him to disagree.

"Then it's a plan," she said.

Shifting into Reverse, she started turning the car around, making a jolting stop when he said, "No."

"Ry…"

"Look, I appreciate your offer. Trust me, it's tempting. But this has gotta happen sooner or later. Might as well be sooner. And if I go—" he briefly considered leaving it at that, but finished "—you won't have to walk in there alone."

She stared at him, taken aback. "You'd do that for me? Why?"

"Call it selfish," he said gruffly, shrugging off the soft note of wonder in her voice. "We obviously feel the same way about it. Might be easier if we walk in together. Three against the rest of 'em, right?"

"Right." Shifting sideways, she studied him, giving Ry the impression she was judging the honesty of his offer. Then she smiled and for the span of seconds he was drawn into her warmth, teased by the subtle scent of her perfume, acutely aware of how close they were. "Thanks. That's nice of you."

A little surprised that he'd let himself get distracted by a simple smile, he tried to sound nonchalant. "You rescued me and Bear. This makes us even."

The closer they got to their destination, though, he began feeling less like a nice guy and more uneasy about his decision to come with her. He couldn't back out, not and feel good about leaving her alone. But when she was parked and out of the car, waiting for him and Bear, he knew he'd made a big mistake.

The whole damned town had to be here and he'd willingly agreed to put himself on public display—his own version of hell on earth.

Chapter Two

Ry and Risa approached a large, sprawling adobe, rock and timber ranch house backed by numerous outbuildings. Despite himself, Ry was impressed. They stopped just shy of the last row of people sitting and standing in huge consecutive circles on the grassy area fronting the main building. A makeshift stage had been set up, and a man holding a microphone was gesturing toward several people seated behind him on the stage, making introductions.

Ry caught the name Aria Declán, saw a tall, willowy, elegant-looking woman rise, smiling, and come up to share the microphone. He also noticed how Risa stiffened, her fingers worrying at her ring.

He lightly touched her shoulder, briefly drawing her eyes to him. She attempted a smile, but her mouth contorted into a grimace instead. The urge to grab her hand

and get them both away was almost overwhelming. Why had she bothered coming when it was obvious she no more wanted to be here than he did?

From their position, almost centered on the stage, they had a good view looking over the heads of the people in the chairs in front of them. But he quickly determined their standing here had been another mistake.

His goal had been to approach quietly, circle the crowd and blend in at the edges, going unnoticed as long as possible. Unfortunately, being a big man with an equally big dog made that impossible. He towered over the people who were seated.

The buzz started at the row nearest them, with heads turning to see who'd arrived so late. Stares followed, murmurs arose, spreading like something contagious throughout the gathering. So much so, Aria, who was in the midst of speaking, had to pause to regain the audience's attention. Seeking the source of the disruption, she zeroed in on her sister and the stranger at her side, and her slightly startled expression matched those of others in the crowd.

Ry took to returning the looks they were getting with a large dose of malice, satisfied when the tactic deterred a good many of the gawkers. Risa, though, looked flushed and tense, her eyes darting around in an attempt to avoid eye contact with anyone and, Ry suspected, gauging her chances of a hasty retreat.

He leaned in close to her ear, so only she could hear, and said, "This seems to be your fifteen seconds of fame."

"Make that *our* fifteen seconds. Your resemblance to Jed hasn't gone unnoticed. And us showing up together—"

"Doesn't it bother you?" Her eyes flitted to the

people around them, swiftly returned to him. "That they're all talking, saying things…"

"No," he said bluntly. "I gave up caring a long time ago what people think of me. But I hate crowds. And this is the last place I'd pick for a family reunion."

"If you wanted one to begin with?"

He answered her with a lift of his shoulders. "What bothers me is you looking like you've been tried and condemned to a life sentence." Taking her hand in his, he clasped her fingers firmly. Her hand felt small and cold in his, the tension radiating from her to him. "Look, your sister knows you got here at least. And she's done with her speech. It looks like they're finishing up. You wanna leave?"

"I hope not." Behind them the deep, rough-edged voice intruded, and they both turned.

With no apology for interrupting, the man who nearly matched Ry in height and build thrust out a hand. "I'm Rafe Garrett. From the looks of you, I'd say I'm your brother."

The name was vaguely familiar because Duran had given him a rundown of his new immediate family. But Ry couldn't see the family resemblance. Instead, the man facing him was obviously Native American. He made no attempt to grasp the offered hand. "I'd say not."

Bear, quiet until now, growled low in his throat. Ry automatically put a hand to the ruff of fur at his neck.

Rafe Garrett, though, was not easily intimidated. He eyed the big dog and then asked, "What's his name?"

"Bear."

The dog rumbled another warning, and Ry tightened his grip.

Rafe studied the dog a moment then went down on

one knee in front of him. He said something deep and quiet in words Ry couldn't decipher before, ever so slowly, lifting a hand to brush Bear's side.

To Ry's annoyance, the growling stopped. Within moments, Bear relaxed and was nuzzling Rafe's hand. So much for his dog's supposed aversion to strangers. In the span of less than an hour, a scrap of a woman and what should have been a threatening stranger had won Bear's friendship with a few words and a pat.

"He's part *lobo,* isn't he?" Rafe asked, straightening.

"No idea," Ry lied. "I doubt you could prove it."

"No reason to." He shifted to look at Risa. A faint smile of recognition touched his mouth. "It's been a long time. Haven't seen you around since high school."

Risa's expression shuttered, but she mustered an answering smile. "That has been a while. A lot's changed since then."

Rafe nodded, adding nothing.

Ry decided he could almost like this guy. He knew the value of silences and didn't seem anxious to push the brotherly bond on him. It was a welcome change from Forrester who apparently felt their being twins automatically meant there was some sort of cosmic link between them. Ry, on the other hand, didn't know what he was supposed to feel.

His predominant urge was to get out now, before he had to confront any more Garrett brothers. But a call of "Hey, Risa" killed any escape plans, and he knew without being told that the man walking up to them had to be another one of those brothers he was trying to avoid. Ry started to question just what kind of group he'd gotten himself mixed up with since the newcomer's dark good looks had obviously been inherited from a

Hispanic mother. Forrester had warned him about the confusion of last names and heritage, but he felt like he needed a scorecard to keep it all straight.

The man greeted Risa with a hug she briefly returned. "Long time no see. It's great to have you back in town," he told her. He flashed a grin, indicating Ry at her side. "And you sure know how to make an entrance." Risa flushed and Ry scowled, but the man overlooked both. Extending a hand he wouldn't withdraw until Ry finally caved in and accepted it, he said, "Cort Morente. You're probably going to get sick of hearing this, but welcome to the family."

"I'm not to the point of thanking anyone for that," Ry said flatly.

Cort flicked a teasing glance at Rafe. "What, you scared him off already?"

"Wouldn't have, if you'd been paying attention and got here first. Greeting all the long-lost relatives is your job," Rafe returned, a dry humor lacing his straight delivery.

"You caught us all by surprise showing up here today," Cort said to Ry. "We knew you were in town last night. The night nurse at the hospital busted you when she told us she'd seen someone who looked like a younger version of Jed." Undeterred by Ry's lack of response, he added, "Duran tried to reach you to tell you about all the partying today, but all he got was your voice mail. I guess you didn't get his messages."

"My cell's dead. I'm not sure I would've shown up otherwise." He glanced at Risa and they exchanged a look that spoke their shared dislike of being in the spotlight.

"I got that." Cort bent to pet Bear, who bared his canines. "And who's this guy?" he asked, unmoved by Bear's display.

"Bear."

Bear continued to growl at Cort, then nipped at him, but his efforts lacked sincerity. Cort respectfully backed off. Ry observed them both, wondering again at the interaction. Maybe Bear was just tired; usually he would have drawn blood by now.

"So, obviously you two have met," Cort said, looking between Risa and Ry. "From what I've heard, half the town saw you walk in together."

"His phone isn't the only thing not working," Risa answered for them both. She gave them the short version of rescuing Ry and Bear after the Land Rover's demise. "I was running so late, I ended up having to drag him along with me to this."

"How are you planning on getting around?" Cort asked Ry.

He and Risa spoke at once.

"I'm driving him—"

"I'll get myself something new—"

They stopped, looked at each other.

"I don't need a driver."

"I didn't need an escort, either."

He glared at her. She held her ground, her eyes challenging him to accept they'd done each other equal favors.

Cort and Rafe exchanged glances, and then Cort asked, "What kind of vehicle do you want? Though none of us is going to be too willing to help you escape so fast."

Thinking that was all the more reason to quicken his departure from Luna Hermosa, Ry gave the easiest answer. "Anything that'll run without blowing up. The cheaper, the better, but big enough for Bear and my gear. Another old Rover or a Jeep would do."

Rafe huffed a laugh. "You been talking to Cort's wife?"

"I've got a really old Jeep, a relic from my days when I was running the canyons, busting drug dealers," Cort admitted. "My wife hates it. And frankly, with four kids, it's just taking up bike, snowboard and skate room in the garage. Laurel would probably pay you to take it off my hands."

"Double, if you take the motorcycle, too," Rafe interjected.

"Don't give her any ideas, because it's not happening. She's gonna have to be satisfied with getting rid of the Jeep. We'll be around tomorrow morning, if you want to come by and take a look at it."

Ry looked at Risa. "If it works for my *driver*."

"As long as it's early," she said, ignoring his emphasis on the word. "I need to put some hours in at the shelter."

"I heard the city council finally approved your women's shelter. Congratulations. I know it was a long, hard battle for your group to get the thing approved in the first place," Cort said. He didn't elaborate further, but from the sympathetic note in his voice and the way Risa's mouth tightened, Ry guessed whatever battles she was fighting weren't quite over. "Laurel and I are available, if you need any help getting set up."

"Thanks," she said shortly. "I think I have it under control."

"Good to hear, but if you change your mind, let us know. Now that we got the transportation issues settled, you guys are staying for the reception, aren't you? I know the rest of the family will want to meet you, Ry."

"Didn't you say you needed to get your gear?" Rafe asked.

Ry hadn't mentioned anything like that, and he almost said as much, until he realized Rafe was giving him a ready excuse to leave. "Yeah, I don't like leaving it on the side of the road any longer than I have to."

"I wouldn't worry—" Cort started, but Rafe shot him a look that could have been a warning and he stopped. "Sure, I understand. We'll all get together when things aren't quite so crazy. I'll see you both tomorrow, then."

Before he could leave them, Risa put a hand on his arm. "Could you please tell Aria I have to go and that I'll call her tomorrow? I'm sorry. I just—I can't be here right now."

"Sure, no worries, okay? She'll understand."

From what he'd gathered of Risa's relationship with her sister, Ry wouldn't have bet that was true. Again, not his business, but it added to the growing list of questions he had about Risa Charez.

After they'd said their goodbyes to Cort, Ry turned to Rafe and started to offer a reluctant thanks for the rescue. But Rafe cut him off. "I hate parties, and in this family they're always finding reasons to have one. Any reason to leave early is good for me." He glanced over the three of them, then added, "You need a ride?"

Ry hesitated, not wanting to be any more in debt to Rafe than he already was.

But Risa preempted his automatic refusal. "My car's pretty small. It's a little crowded with the three of us."

"My truck's more than big enough," Rafe said. "Let me tell my wife what's going on. I'll meet you back here."

"I think I'll go on ahead," Risa said when Rafe had left.

Suspecting she wanted to escape before any of her family found her, he nodded. "I'll meet you back by the Rover?"

"Sure, no problem," she said with a genuine smile.

"I'm only temporarily ceding my status as your personal driver to Rafe."

As he watched her walk away, small, proud, stubborn, closed off from everyone she knew, Ry told himself the last thing he needed was to get tangled up in the middle of her issues. The last thing he needed was to care.

He was struck, though, by the feeling that whether he wanted it or not, he had already put himself in a place with her that was going to be damned hard to leave.

"It's only for the night," Risa assured Ry yet again as he and Bear reluctantly followed her into her father's house.

After they'd rescued his gear, Rafe had asked Ry where he was staying, and it was then she'd learned that he'd camped out the night before and planned to do the same for as many days as he was in Luna Hermosa, despite the inconveniences and the chilly fall weather.

They arranged to drop most of Ry's gear off at Cort's house, since Ry intended to come back the next day to look at the Jeep. Needing to get back to his wife and twin toddlers, Rafe left Risa with the job of convincing Ry that one night in a real bed wouldn't be as torturous as he apparently thought it would be.

She'd done her best over the last several hours, all through dinner at the local diner, and now, standing in the darkened foyer. At least they were alone, her father and the rest of them not yet returned from dinner with Aria and her family at Rancho Pintada.

"We can't be that far from the river." Ry started up his protests again.

"I am not hauling you two to some godforsaken spot by the river or anywhere else tonight. Most of your stuff is at Cort's anyway," Risa said firmly. "My father's been a foster parent since before I was born. He's got plenty of extra room, and he never minds making space for one more person."

"A foster parent." His flat tone didn't inspire confidence that she was going to be able to keep him here.

"Yes, he's fostering two children now."

"Great." Ry took a step back toward the door, and she wondered if he even realized he was doing it. At his side, Bear hugged close to his leg, and he automatically reached down to scratch the dog's neck. "Look, this isn't a good idea."

"Why not? If you're worried about what my father will say—"

"I grew up in foster homes." He abruptly cut her off. "I'm not interested in reliving the experience."

His admission touched that part of her that had spent years trying to help those with broken lives repair the damage. Knowing the foster system all too well, she suspected he had likely been a victim of the darker side of it.

"My father isn't like that." She spoke quietly, the way she did to the women and children she worked with, women who'd been beaten, demeaned, neglected, threatened. In Ry's hardened expression and sudden retreat, she saw the faces of the abandoned women and children she knew so well. "He and my mother were good foster parents. My father still is. Cort's oldest son, Tommy, lived with Dad for a while before Cort and Laurel adopted him. You can ask them, ask Tommy, how he was treated."

A touch frustrated when she continued to get the stone-faced stare, she tried appealing to his common sense. "Ry—please. This isn't a lifetime commitment.

It's just one night. Besides—" in an attempt to lighten the situation, she tried a small smile "—if you're going to go through with this family reunion of yours, especially with Jed, you're going to need a good night's rest."

His mouth twisted. "I think I can manage a meeting with one sick old man."

"You don't know Jed. He'd pick a fight with the devil if it meant getting what he wanted. Jed's a survivor."

"Tough and mean. We oughta get along just fine."

"Probably. You remind me of him, in some ways."

"Tough and mean?" he repeated, a touch of amusement in his raised brow.

"Maybe that, too," she teased. "But I was thinking that you're a survivor."

The flint returned to his eyes. "It comes easy when you don't have a choice."

"That can be a good thing, though getting there isn't always the easiest."

His hand moved restlessly against Bear's back again and his only response was a tense silence.

"I'll show you to your room," she said finally. She led him to a room across the hall from hers. "The bathroom's to the left. Kitchen is near the den if you get hungry in the night."

"Can I get a bowl of water for Bear?"

"Oh, sure. We have dog food, too." She told him where all of that was in lieu of taking him to the kitchen to get it for him. He didn't seem to want help of any kind and to resent having to ask for the help he'd gotten.

"So." She shuffled a little, then decided to get out of his way for the night. "You have everything you need?"

"Yeah. I'm good."

Not wanting to leave him yet, but wanting—what? Something she couldn't define and felt silly trying to, she smiled a good-night and spun on her heel. He didn't move.

Clasping the doorknob to her room she paused. His dominating presence emanated close and warm behind her. Her hand dropped from the door but she didn't turn around. He was so close she heard him breathing, felt the rise and fall of his chest; was surrounded by the musky, male scent of him.

Her breath quickened along with the beat of her heart. He said nothing, but stood, in silence, breathing deeply, the heat of his body reaching the cold in her.

Finally, she turned. He didn't touch her, instead letting his eyes take that role. Now shadowed, mysterious yet open, his gaze spoke what he could not. "Thanks," he said quietly.

It wasn't an eloquent or effusive expression of gratitude, but it was simple and honest, and spoke everything she needed to know. "You're welcome."

There were a few beats of silence when they looked at each other and then, slower than a rain-bereft river, Ry very gently brushed a stray wisp of hair from her cheek.

The sweet warmth of his brief touch spread like a comforting cocoon down and around her entire body, enveloping her at the same time his arms closed around her. With a sigh, she relaxed against him, like summer grass bending to the will of the wind; he held her, rocking her gently with him, holding her close and it was like coming home.

She laid her head on his shoulder, and they stood in the darkened hallway between his room and hers, holding each other for a small eternity, as though yesterday and tomorrow didn't exist.

Chapter Three

Never had a short drive seemed so long.

Risa glanced at Ry, getting the same view of his profile she'd had since they'd left her father's house for Cort's. His face was shadowed by the beat-up leather hat he wore, his expression unreadable, but she could almost believe he was frozen in that position—eyes fixed straight ahead, stiffly upright—if not for the flex of his fingers against Bear's fur.

He'd been this way, sullen and uncommunicative, since he'd awakened her at the crack of dawn, wanting to leave for Cort's house. She'd refused to accommodate him until she'd fortified herself with a shower and coffee. The only benefit to being rousted out of bed at that hour was that no one else had been awake when they'd left, giving Risa the chance to put off explaining Ry and the whole mess yesterday to her father,

Instead, she left her father a short note, saying she'd call him later.

"You're lucky Cort has four kids who probably wake him up before sunrise, too." She finally broke the extended silence as she parked in the driveway of the large ranch-style home. "Otherwise, I would have made you wait."

"You did anyway," he grumbled.

"Next time you can walk," she shot back and had her door open and one leg out before his hand on her shoulder stopped her.

Reluctantly, she turned to look at him. He rubbed a hand over the back of his neck, blew out a breath and said, "I'm sorry. All this—" he gestured vaguely around them "—is getting to me. I need to get somewhere I can think."

Somewhere alone, she heard loudly and clearly. She tried not to remember last night, the moment of communion and tenderness between them that today felt like a dream of other people. And it might as well have been a dream. There was no reason to believe anything about it had been real or more than two people comforting each other after a hard day.

"Then let's go get the Jeep, and you can be on your way," she told him instead of other things she wanted to say, other questions she wanted to ask. Not waiting for him to agree, she slipped out of his hold and the car.

He left Bear in the backseat after she warned him three of Cort's kids were under seven years old and unaccustomed to unfriendly animals. The bit about unfriendly animals came out a little sharper than she'd intended and with a warning look at him.

The corner of his mouth lifted. "Are you saying I should wait in the car with him?"

"Depends. Do you promise not to bite?"

Something sparked in his eyes, shifting the hazel color closer to golden brown than deep river green. "Depends on the circumstances."

"I'm not going to touch that one. Let's just agree these aren't the circumstances," she said, then flushed at the smile he didn't try too hard to hide.

The smile vanished moments later when Cort opened the door to them. His arms full of a giggling little boy with a mess of dark hair and a cheeky grin, Cort gestured them inside with a tip of his head before stooping to let the boy wriggle out of his hold. "Excuse the chaos," he said as he led them into the living room, his son racing ahead. "You caught us in our after breakfast attempt to get organized. Laurel and I promised the kids we'd go riding today."

The attractive blond woman perched on the edge of the couch, fastening the end of a braid for a little girl, looked up and smiled. "Okay, all done. Go and find your sister, Sophie, and tell her to help you find your pink sweatshirt," she said, kissing her daughter's cheek. "And take Quin with you. I'll be there in a few minutes." Sophie shot a curious look at the new arrivals and then darted off toward a back room, her brother in tow. Laurel got up and moved to Cort's side.

"We were sorry neither of you could stay for the reception yesterday," Laurel said after Cort had introduced her to Risa and Ry. "I know Aria missed having you there, Risa." She turned to Ry. "And we've all been looking forward to meeting you. Does this mean you'll be here for the wedding?"

Risa exchanged a look with Ry, and his blank expression told her he was as clueless as she. "Wedding?" she asked.

"Duran's getting married on New Year's Eve. Didn't he tell you?"

"No," Ry said grimly, "he didn't."

"He and Lia just told the rest of us yesterday," Cort intervened. "I doubt he's had the chance to say anything to you."

"I'll have to see how things go, especially with work. I wasn't planning on sticking around that long."

"Long enough to meet the rest of the family, we hope," Cort said.

Ry answered with a shift of his shoulders and muttered, "Yeah, it looks like it," and it was all Risa could do not to elbow him in the ribs, prodding him to more of a response.

"I'll call Duran," he said finally. "And I was planning on stopping by the hospital again."

It wasn't exactly a promise, and fell far short of what Cort wanted to hear. But Risa could tell it was more than Ry wanted to give and the best his brother was going to get for now.

The undercurrent of tension between the two men hummed just below the surface for the rest of the visit. It aggravated her raw nerves, and by the time Cort and Ry had settled on a selling price for the Jeep and loaded Ry's gear into the vehicle, she was more than ready to leave.

"You sure about camping out?" Cort asked as Ry let Bear into the front seat of the Jeep. "There's plenty of room at the ranch, or at Josh and Eliana's. Sawyer and Maya have an extra bedroom, too," he added, mentioning his older brother and his wife, "although you won't find much peace and quiet there with the three kids."

"No, thanks," Ry said shortly.

"Cell phone service isn't the most reliable once you get out of town. Somebody should probably know where you're staying, in case we need to find you. I'd follow you myself if we didn't already have plans with the kids. I can call Sawyer or Cruz—"

"I'll do it," Risa interrupted because Cort wasn't going to let this go and she was certain Ry's response was going to be a flat-out refusal bordering on rude.

From the way his expression darkened and the glare he flicked her, she wasn't too sure she wouldn't be getting the same treatment.

Cort, eyeing his brother, then her, looked doubtful. "You sure? There's no need for you to make the trip alone."

"It's not a problem." She looked directly at Ry. "Is it?"

He took several long seconds to answer. "I guess not. Are you ready to go?"

She was, and yet, after saying her goodbyes to Cort and starting after the Jeep, she mentally crossed her fingers and hoped she wasn't going to regret allying herself with Ry Kincaid.

"Go ahead, say it." Slamming the last tent stake into the ground, Ry straightened and faced Risa where she sat on a rock several feet away, watching him. She arched a questioning brow, and he added, "Tell me what a rude son of a bitch I am and get it over with."

When her mouth stayed stubbornly pursed in a tight line, he blew out a frustrated breath. "I'd rather you cussed me out than give me the silent treatment."

"Oh, this from the man who's an expert at it. You know, Ry, I don't know what it is you do for a living, but I hope it doesn't involve personal interaction with anyone other than your dog, because you suck at it."

"Yeah, I do." He thought about it for a moment then tacked on, gruffly, "Never had much chance to practice."

She softened at that, lowering the arms she'd had crossed over her breasts. "Why did you come here? If you're so uncomfortable with the idea of having a family, why bother acknowledging them at all?"

"I was—curious." The word was inadequate to describe the feelings that had lured him to Luna Hermosa, and he had no experience in talking about emotions. Risa, though, he wanted her to understand, because if anyone he'd ever met could, maybe it was her. He walked over and sat down next to her, the song of the river to their backs, the sigh of the wind through the trees its accompaniment. "Duran, he was adopted when he was a baby by people who cared. They didn't want me. I ended up adopted by the Kincaids, but about the only thing they gave me was a name."

"What happened?"

"They split up when I was two. I don't know much about it except the state decided after that I wasn't theirs anymore. I wasn't anybody's. I got bounced around foster homes. Most of them were okay. A couple of them, not as good. And the last one—"

Her breath caught and, very gently, she touched his hand. "Ry—"

"The guy, the foster *father,* his way of proving he was a big man was abusing the kids his wife kept taking in. I guess the kids were too scared to say anything about it, and the social worker didn't care enough to figure it out. I didn't last long. There was this girl. She was maybe twelve—I couldn't just watch it happen. He ended up in the hospital for a week. I spent almost a year in juvenile detention." He shook his head sharply, warding off any show of pity she might have made. "I don't think about it anymore. That's done with."

"Don't you?"

"No," he said firmly, unsure if he meant it but not willing to admit it if he didn't. "I was sixteen when I got out. I ditched the social worker and hitchhiked to Colorado. Got lucky there. I met a guy who ran an out-fitting business. He gave me a job, made me finish school. Been on my own ever since." After a pause, he added, "Wilderness guide," and at her blank look said, "That's what I do for a living."

She smiled a little. "Ah, that explains your allergic reaction to real beds and hot showers. I'll bet you're good at it."

"Good enough. I get my fair share of work. Might be time, though, to stop working for someone else."

"You mean starting your own business?"

"I've thought about it. But not in Colorado. I need a new base. Arizona, Montana—maybe even New Mexico. There's a guy here I've done some freelance work for who's been running the river and doing wild-erness trips for longer than any man should be alive. He's older than dirt and about as stubborn as that boulder over there," he said, nodding to a huge rock jutting up in the middle of the river. "I'm thinking he may be about ready to pass the torch."

"Sounds like a possibility. But if it doesn't work out, there are still probably some good opportunities here for that kind of work," she said in a tone that didn't commit her to any opinion about the idea of him staying in New Mexico. Flattening her palms on the rock behind her, she leaned back on her arms, her face tilted toward the warmth of the sun. "So, tell me about Bear. How'd you two end up together?"

Ry glanced to the river, where his dog was happily

exploring the shoreline. "About three years ago, I was doing a job in Wyoming, one of those boot camps for kids in trouble—"

"Really? Wow, there goes my picture of you as the bad-tempered recluse."

"Interesting mix of insult and compliment there. Anyway, I found Bear in a ditch. He was a little thing then. Someone had beaten him and thrown him in there." The memory still had the power to clench his hands into fists. "I took him with me, got him fixed up and since then I've had a big furry roommate."

Ry turned to find her studying him, as if she were weighing what she knew about him and what she'd imagined and trying to reconcile the two.

Most women annoyed him with their attempts to try to figure him out, probe past his toughened outer shell to pick apart what lay underneath and attempt to get him to talk about it. Which was why he defined all his relationships in terms of days, having the kind of sex that meant nothing, with the least emotions involved as possible.

But Risa provoked a completely different response in him; one he didn't know what to do with. Not that he didn't want her—he did. She was hotter than hell without even trying. In boots and faded jeans with a rip across the thigh, and a zip-up hooded sweatshirt, her hair ruffled, she wasn't trying today. Yet imagining himself slowly drawing down that zipper and exposing everything beneath was more enticing to him than any deliberate attempt on her part to dress seductively.

He could still feel her on his body from last night when he'd held her. He could have had her there, and she would have let it happen. Except, for the first time, he'd actually *thought* about it, and the thinking had made him uncomfortable, leaving him sure he'd be hurting her in some way by treating her like every other woman.

Instead, he'd just held her, and that had been a first, too.

"You hungry?" he said abruptly, on his feet and half-way to the Jeep before she had a chance to answer.

"Since breakfast was a cup of coffee I barely finished, yes. Are you offering me lunch?"

"If you give me time to catch it."

Risa eyed him warily. "Define *it*. And if it involves you slaughtering something with your bare hands, the answer's no."

"Do trout fall into that category?" he asked over his shoulder, busy digging his tackle out of the back of the Jeep.

"No, I like trout. Although I have to say, this is the first time anyone's offered to catch and cook me lunch. You are cooking it, right? This isn't going to be some mountain-man form of sushi?"

Ry laughed. "Even I'm not that uncivilized."

She followed him as he started toward the river. "Can I help with something?"

"I'm good." He flashed a grin. "You can just watch and be impressed by my amazing skills."

Rolling her eyes, she left him to the fish and went to greet Bear, who'd come running toward them. She and his dog wandered along the edge of the river, stopping here and there to explore, while Ry tried to concentrate on catching lunch and not on how comfortable it was having her there, how he even liked it.

"Tell me about this shelter of yours," he prompted a little over an hour later when they were partway through their meal.

Fidgeting with her food for a moment, she finally said, "I'm one of those social workers you like so much," and slanted a look at him, almost as if she expected his censure. When he only nodded, some of the tension left her shoulders. "I work for a nonprofit group that operates shelters for women and their children. They've got several of them throughout the state, but there's not much in this area. The closest is Albuquerque, and that's three hours too far if you need help right away. So they asked me if I'd take on setting one up here."

"And you couldn't say no? Because I get the impression you like being here less than I do."

A smile touched her mouth. "I don't think that's possible." Sobering, she looked away. "No—I couldn't say no. I owe them."

Whatever the debt was, she seemed reluctant to talk about it. Ry was ready to let it go, respecting her desire to protect her secrets, but with a small sigh, she put down her plate and offered him more.

"They helped me when I didn't have anyone else. I ran away from home when I was sixteen. I ended up in Albuquerque and spent a few nights on the street before I was lucky enough to find the shelter. If I hadn't—" With a quick, jerky motion, she dragged her fingers through her hair. "Well, things would have turned out a lot differently."

"What were you running away from?"

"My family." His surprise must have shown, because her mouth quirked at the corner in a sardonic facsimile of a smile. "If you're here any time at all, you'll find out I'm the Charez's black-sheep daughter. I was always in trouble as a kid. I ran pretty wild.

Then I was gone for a year, and I never contacted anyone to let them know where I was or even that I was okay. When I finally came back home, I didn't stay long, because I got tired of everyone telling me how horrible and ungrateful I was for putting my parents through all that. They're the saints and I'm the sinner and I don't think I'm ever going to be forgiven for what I did."

Ry didn't want to belittle her feelings, but he didn't understand them, either. "That was a long time ago. What's it matter now? Everyone does stupid things when they're a teenager."

"Not Aria," she said and then flushed. She began twisting her ring. "Everyone in my family has always been better than me. My parents were loving and caring. They fostered all those kids, and a lot of them had special needs. And Aria was the good girl, smart and beautiful, always involved in some charity project. She still is—look at the children's ranch. She got the whole town supporting her on that. I, on the other hand, have managed in the week I've been back to get a whole lot of people mad at me because they don't want my kind of shelter in their backyards. On top of that, I've upset my father because I won't talk to him about why I left, and I've aggravated Aria, and probably most of your family, too, because I managed to miss her big day."

He waited for her to wind down, then deliberately took his time putting his plate aside. He resettled himself with his back to the rock, legs stretched out in front of him, and looked at her. "That's a lot of drama for one week," he finally said.

Risa stared at him, and Ry wondered if he'd been too dismissive. Then she started laughing, and although there was a brittle quality to it, there was also an appreciation for his matter-of-fact observation. "I guess it is."

"Look—I don't know much about your family and what they have or haven't done, and I don't really care. All that crap that happened with you was like, what? Thirteen, fourteen years ago? If people haven't gotten over it by now, screw 'em. It's not their business anyway."

"You've obviously never lived long in a small town," she said with a wince.

"You care too much what other people think. Why'd you come back if you knew this is what you'd be putting up with?"

"The only way to get rid of the ghosts of the past is to confront them. That's the social-worker speech I give my clients, anyway. I thought that was what I was doing. Turns out they're not ghosts, though. They're still alive and kicking."

"Because you won't let them die," he persisted. "You can't change what happened. Accept it and move on."

She shook her head, turned to look at the river but not before he glimpsed the glint of unshed tears. "Sometimes that's not possible."

He didn't know how to comfort her; there'd been too few times in his life when anyone had offered it to him for it to be familiar. Anything he said now would probably be the wrong thing, so he said nothing.

His silence, though, seemed to be the catalyst for shifting her mood. After a few minutes, she straightened her shoulders, rolled her neck a half twist and faced him again. "I wish I didn't have to leave."

"Then don't. Bear won't mind." He nodded to where his dog was now stretched out in his usual napping place when they were camping, half in and half out of the tent.

"I notice you didn't include yourself in that," she said with a smile. Shaking her head to show him she didn't expect an open invitation from him, she arched her back, stretching in the dappling of sunlight that shone through the stand of pines. "I need to get back. I've got a lot of work to finish before I can get the shelter up and running. But I know where to find you if I want another fish dinner. If you're planning on sticking around for a while, that is."

"For a while." Levering to his feet, he held out a hand to help her up, keeping her hand in his for a few moments longer than necessary. "If you need to get away…I won't mind, either."

They were close, no more than a step away from being in each other's arms, and he could tell from the slow flush sweeping her face and her quickened breath, his proximity affected her. The tip of her tongue darted over her lower lip, focusing his eyes there. He wanted to kiss her and if he made the smallest shift forward—

She stepped back. "Thanks for lunch. Call me if you need anything else." Hesitating, she quickly added, "I hope we'll see each other again, before you decide to leave."

"Count on it." He let her go, watched as she got into her car and started the engine. But the sound of the motor spurred him to stride quickly to the driver's door. "Risa—" He leaned his hands against the roof and let their eyes lock. "I don't know about your qualifications for local sainthood. But smart and beautiful—you got that covered."

Her lips parted then, closed and she only smiled. Then she was gone, and he was alone again. He'd never been bothered by it before, never thought about it before. Except now, without her there, instead of familiar solitude he felt an emptiness; something lost that he didn't know he'd had until she took it with her.

He didn't know what to call it, so he gave it her name. And when the chill of night set in, he brought it out of his memories and with it brought a little of her warmth back into the cold places of his heart.

Chapter Four

Risa had planned to get to the shelter much earlier in the day, but had no regrets for the time she'd spent with Ry at his riverside campsite.

Her regrets came when she unlocked the door to the house she'd fought half the town and most of the city council to get, and the pressures of trying to get the shelter up and running came back tenfold. The place was a mess. Knowing she was largely on her own in dealing with it, she almost wished she'd stayed with Ry.

After they had shared confidences, she'd felt more at ease with him and Bear by the river than she had since she'd come home.

Blunt often to the point of rudeness, and with his share of rough edges, Ry Kincaid hadn't endeared himself to anyone in town, his family included. But the things about him that put off others attracted her. He didn't make apologies for who he was or what he'd done, and he didn't care what others thought of him. Her past sins didn't interest him, either, and she considered that one of his most attractive traits.

That, coupled with his rugged good looks—muscled, tanned arms, ripped abs and jeans worn so long they molded to a hard backside…Risa stopped herself. She didn't need to get sidetracked by him. She had work to do and lots of it, and fantasizing about Ry Kincaid wasn't going to get it done.

Walking through the empty living room, kitchen and bedrooms, she wondered how long it would take her to make the place livable. She estimated weeks, maybe, until she opened the garage door and disaster greeted her.

Floor to ceiling furniture, boxes of dishes, pots and pans, linens, a couple of TVs, a freezer, clothes, toys and even some usable drapes packed the small space. They were all donations, largely thanks to Aria's efforts.

Aria… She'd yet to explain her hasty exit from yesterday's ceremony. Her sister deserved that much. Striding back through the house to where she'd tossed her purse, she grabbed her cell phone. Aria answered on the second ring.

"I wanted to say I'm sorry for yesterday," Risa said. "I'd planned to be there. But it got complicated."

"I heard. It's okay, really. I know you wanted to be there, and that's all that matters." There was a pause, then Aria asked, "Are you okay?"

"Yes, fine. Why?"

"Dad told me Ry Kincaid spent the night but that you and he were gone early this morning. And then Cort said you'd gone off with Ry alone to some remote campsite. We were all a little worried."

"There's nothing to worry about. I followed him out there, he made me lunch, and then I came back to do some work at the shelter. That's the end of it."

"He didn't make a very good impression on Cort," Aria persisted. "And from what I saw of him, he looks a little dangerous."

A sudden wave of defensiveness came over Risa. "Ry's not concerned with impressing anyone. And before you say it, I know he resembles Jed, but he's nothing like him."

"How can you know that already?"

"I know enough." Frustrated, Risa shifted her phone to the other ear and began to pace. "He's not what you think."

"I see." An awkward silence fell, and then Risa could almost hear her sister make the effort to drop the subject of Ry Kincaid. "So, what are you up to there?"

"I just took a look at all of the donations you managed to get," Risa said, grateful that Aria wanted to end what had become an uncomfortable discussion. "How can I thank you? There's so much stuff crammed in the garage, I don't know where to start with arranging it all."

"I could come over and give you a hand. Cruz and Mateo are perfectly content watching a football game this afternoon. Well, it's more like Cruz is watching the game and Mateo is watching his daddy. I'm just spinning my wheels here."

Risa laughed. "I know that's something you're not so good at."

"So, will you let me help you? I'll just be a technician, promise. No ideas or suggestions."

"Like that's going to happen. But I'd appreciate any help I can get. It's a little overwhelming."

It was all the encouragement Aria needed. "Great, I'll be right over."

True to her word, Aria arrived in less than fifteen minutes. Despite her sister's promise, Risa sensed Aria's struggle to stop herself every time she was tempted to overrun her and take control, as she'd always done growing up. But now her big sister was making a genuine effort to respect Risa's opinions, wishes and tastes, and Risa in turn appreciated it.

They managed to work relatively peacefully together the rest of the day and into the evening, moving the lighter pieces of furniture and boxes into the house, unpacking all the kitchen supplies and hanging a set of bright checked café curtains in the kitchen window.

"That's it," Risa said after they'd made the final adjustments to the curtains. "You've been at it for hours. Cruz and Mateo must be lonesome for you, not to mention starving. Let's call it a day."

Aria stepped down from the stool she was using and looked around them. "There's so much more to do. Didn't you say you had women and children already waiting in line to come here?"

"I'll get it done. I'll just need some help with the dressers and beds."

"I'm sure Cruz or any of his brothers would be glad to help you. Or you could ask Ry," Aria added with a pointed glance. "Whom, by the way, you've done a good job of avoiding talking about all day."

The old blue and white linoleum floor became suddenly fascinating. "I haven't been avoiding it."

"Yes. You have. And I'm starting to wonder why."

"Well, if I have, it's only because I don't want you to make any assumptions."

"About what? I'm not judging you, Risa, no matter what you might think. I've never done that."

"Everyone's done that. You did your share of reminding me how much I'd screwed up after I'd left and come back."

"Maybe I did, but it was because I saw how much it hurt Mom and Dad." Aria made a frustrated gesture. "We always do this."

"I know," Risa said, the fight draining out of her. She felt guilty and a little sad that she'd let her defensiveness about the past come between her and Aria again. "I'm sorry. I don't want to do this."

"Me, either," Aria said, putting a hand on her arm. "So let's forget it. Tell me more about Ry."

"You never give up, do you?" Resigned to satisfying some of her sister's curiosity, Risa gave her an abbreviated version of what she knew about Ry's history, leaving out the worst of what Ry had told her about his years as a foster child. "He's still a loner, but I can understand why. It's hard for him to accept he's got family now."

Aria didn't respond right away, and Risa resisted the urge to squirm under her sister's appraising gaze. "You seem to have gotten to know him pretty well in a short time."

"Not really." Risa dismissed the idea, not wanting to leave Aria with the impression she and Ry had developed any sort of bond. "I'm not likely to, either. He's leaving. And, as far as he's concerned, the sooner the better."

But hours later, looking out her bedroom window at the zillion sparkling stars embedded in a cobalt sky on the clear fall night, she thought she might have lied about her connection to Ry.

In her mind's eye, she imagined herself back at his campsite, the scent of wood smoke in the air, the cool river breeze kissing her face, the sounds of water and wind. More strongly, she envisioned Ry, perhaps now asleep under the open sky. She pictured herself enfolded in his arms, and in her dreams it was the sanctuary she'd long tried to find.

Ry lay on his back, sleeping bag tossed open, unable to sleep.

He'd resorted to staring at the midnight sky while he tried not to dwell on tomorrow and the meeting he planned with Jed Garrett. He tried harder not to think about Risa.

It would make his life a lot easier if he could dismiss whatever he felt for her as simple lust. But it was more complicated than that. He liked being around her. She didn't let him cow her with his abrasiveness or his blunt speaking, and without prying encouraged him to tell her things he'd never revealed to anyone else. It was a strange feeling, good and unsettling at the same time.

And he had no clue what to do about it.

He thought about how she'd said she wanted to stay with him rather than go back into town and wished he'd said something to keep her longer, wanted, too, the right words to make her smile, but without the shadows that kept it from being full and joyful.

At the meandering river's edge, beneath the spectacular array of stars, he wondered how he might make that happen.

The next morning, Ry stood in the doorway of a hospital room looking into eyes that could have been his.

"You gonna just stand there and stare, boy?"

Giving way to a compulsion to meet his biological father seemed like a far worse idea now than it had last night when he'd reluctantly surrendered to it. But he was here, the man was awake, and he might as well satisfy his curiosity and get it over with. He stepped into the room but kept his distance.

"I figured it was time we met," he said.

Jed stared him up and down. What might have been satisfaction crossed his features. "No doubt you're my boy. I wondered about Duran. Guess he takes after your mama."

"Guess you wouldn't know," Ry said. "Duran said you don't remember her."

"Don't go judgin' me. From what your brothers tell me about you, I'd bet my ranch you've had more than your share of women you don't recall. I just got unlucky that night."

The words hit him with the force of a blow. But how could the old man hurt him now? Ry had been unwanted from the start. He didn't expect Jed Garrett to care about him anymore than the woman who'd given him away.

The old man must have seen something in Ry's expression, because his face hardened. "I can't change what's past. Like I told Duran, I never knew about the two of you, and I'm not gonna pretend I would have wanted to know back then. If you're wantin' to wallow in what's done and over with, then get out now, because I ain't got the time or the stomach for it. We can start from here or not at all." Slowly, Jed stretched out a hand.

Ry stayed in place, looking at the man with a face so similar to his own, overwhelmed by the sensation that if he accepted Jed's offering, he'd be taking a step that would irrevocably change his life. It shook him, made him question who he was and what he wanted.

But he took that step because if he didn't, it would mean admitting he was afraid.

His gaze steady, on Jed, Ry grasped his father's hand with a firm hold and held it for a long moment that for all its intensity could have been a lost lifetime.

It ended abruptly when a nurse walked in.

"Oh, perfect," the nurse said. "I'm completely swamped this morning. You can walk him."

Ry frowned. "What?"

"Well, you are his son, *obviously*. You can help him with his morning walk."

"I don't think so."

"The only way to recover from a broken hip is to strengthen the muscles around it. To do that, he has to walk, and he can't do it alone." With that, she turned to Jed, ignoring his cursing and grumbling while she instructed Ry on helping her get his father to his feet with the IV line intact.

Reluctantly, Ry obeyed, all the while wondering how the hell he could get out of this. Meeting the old man was one thing; taking on the role of personal caregiver was way out of bounds. He had no desire to get this up close and personal with a stranger, related to him or not.

"Grab that gown and tie it in back," the nurse said. "No one around here wants to see that much of him." When Ry recoiled, she frowned impatiently. "I don't have time for your macho nonsense. Just do it."

Ry muttered a curse and earned himself a tight smile from Jed. Ry tentatively took hold of the ties at Jed's back and pulled them into the kind of knots he used to tie gear onto rafts.

"You're definitely my boy," Jed said, a touch of pride coloring his voice. "And quit talkin' about me like I'm not here, woman," he added, fixing a scowl on the hovering nurse.

"The two of you aren't making this easy. Now take his arm," she told Ry, "and walk him down the hall and back. That's enough for now. He'll need another session this afternoon."

"I'll take that one." The slightly bemused voice came from the doorway. When Ry and Jed looked up, Jed grunted and shook his head. "If they staffed this place right, none of you'd be doin' this." He glowered at the nurse. She frowned back, snapped out another order for Jed to walk and then left them. "You met your brother yet, Sawyer?" Jed asked the newcomer.

"No, I haven't had the chance." Sawyer came over and held out a hand to Ry. At least Ry could see some family connection between two of his brothers, in the strong resemblance between Sawyer and Cort. "I'm looking forward to talking to you later," Sawyer said. He glanced between Jed and Ry, fixing on Ry. "Rough morning?"

Ry looked away.

Jed gave a derisive snort. "Damned nurses expect everyone else to do their job."

"How about I give you a hand?" Sawyer offered. He took one of Jed's arms and Ry the other and between the two of them, they carefully helped Jed navigate into the hallway.

Ry fantasized about jumping out the window while Sawyer made small talk with Jed about the grandkids and ranch business. When he knew Sawyer had a firm hold on Jed, he started searching out the nearest exit. He had to get out. He'd never had a panic attack before, but this feeling that he was suffocating had to come close.

"Maya and I would like to have you to dinner soon," Sawyer said. Ry was on the brink of telling him no when his cell phone barked in his pocket.

Some techie's idea of a joke, it was the ring tone that had come with the phone and he'd never bothered to figure out how to change it. At least he'd remembered to charge the phone the night he spent at Risa's house. Whoever it was, he or she was his escape.

"Ry?" Risa's voice, a little hesitant, sounded like heaven to him. "I was wondering, are you busy for the next hour or so?"

"What's up?"

"Well, I'm at the shelter and there's some furniture I need moved. It's pretty heavy, and I can't do it myself. If you've got time—"

"What's the address?"

"What?" She sounded startled.

"The address. I can be there in ten."

"Oh… Are you in town?"

"Yeah, tell me where you are." She rattled off a street and a number and committing it to memory, he told her, "I'll see you in a few minutes," then turned to Sawyer and said, "I gotta go. He's okay with you, right?"

Brows drawn, Sawyer nodded. "Yes, but—"

"Later. I'll be in touch." Stepping away from Sawyer and Jed, he faced his father. He found himself at a loss for words. Everything that came to mind sounded like a cliché and didn't begin to explain his conflicted feelings.

Jed spared him the effort. With a nod and an even look that held no malice, he said, "You know where to find me."

"Yeah, I do." With that Ry spun on his heel and almost sprinted for the door.

Chapter Five

Ry fit the dresser into place against the bedroom wall with a last push. Keeping his hands braced against it, he glanced over his shoulder at Risa. "You aren't gonna change your mind about this one, are you?"

She laughed, but a little sheepishly. He wouldn't have asked if she hadn't three times changed her mind about the placement of two beds and a very large chest. "No, I promise. This one stays there."

"Good thing, because if it needed moving, I was gonna make you do it yourself." He straightened and swiped his forearm against his temple. "Any water left in the cooler?"

"Water, diet soda and cheap beer, take your pick. And I ran out before you got here and grabbed some sandwiches. I don't know about you, but I'm ready for a break."

He nodded, following her into the kitchen, where

she'd left the supplies. They took their lunch out to the back porch, sitting on the steps to eat and enjoy the fall sunshine, feeding Bear his share when he ambled over to check out what they'd brought.

They'd been at it for three hours straight—painting, cleaning and moving furniture—and Risa could feel it in her neck and shoulders as she leaned back on her hands and stretched out her legs. Two of the four bedrooms were nearly done, though, and they'd made a good start on the third. It was definitely progress, and she owed it to Ry.

"Thanks again for coming over," she told him, adding before she realized what she was revealing, "I couldn't have gotten half as much done without help, but I didn't feel comfortable asking anyone else."

"No problem." He tossed the remains of his sandwich to Bear, then reached for another beer. "It was a good excuse to get away from the scene at the hospital."

"How did that go, with Jed?"

"It was…I don't know. What I expected and some things I didn't."

"You don't have to tell me."

"It's not that. I don't know what to think right now. The old man, he's as tough and mean as you said. But he doesn't pretend to be anything else, and he says what he wants straight out. I like him for that. The rest of 'em—" Shaking his head, he stared out in front of him, a muscle twitching along his jaw. "Sawyer's as bad as Cort, wanting us all to get together and act like it means something. Just because we've got the same father, it doesn't make us family."

"No, but they're still your brothers." He shrugged in response, and she dropped it. He needed to set his own timetable for dealing with his family. Besides, she could hardly claim to be an expert at family relations considering her own uneasy relationships with her father and sister.

She changed the subject. "So, what do you think my chances are of getting this place in shape before Christmas? I know of at least two women in this area that I would love to be able to offer a room here today."

He slanted a look in her direction, acknowledging the sudden change in the conversation. "Depends on whether I'm your only help. You've got a lot of things around here that need fixing."

"That's what the building inspector said," she confessed. "But the group I work for doesn't have a lot of resources, and I needed something cheap. This place has a lot of room, a big yard for the kids. It's in a quiet neighborhood, and it's got potential."

"I don't know about potential. Problems are more like it."

"Pessimist," she accused, lightly bumping his shoulder with hers.

"Realist," he came back. Getting to his feet, he offered her a hand up. "Walk me through it again, and I'll give you a list."

Leaving Bear basking in the sun in the fenced backyard, they spent the better part of an hour inspecting every room of the house. Risa made notes as Ry pointed out several things from the roof to the walk-out basement that needed attention and weren't likely to pass muster with the building inspector.

"Okay, maybe Christmas next year," Risa muttered when they'd finished and were standing in the living room. The line of tall windows at the front of the house, bare of any coverings, let through a flood of light, emphasizing the overall shabbiness of the room and picking out in detail every issue that Ry had found. She rubbed at the spot between her eyes, feeling the start of a headache.

"Having second thoughts?"

"No, this is the best location in town for what I need. I've just got to figure out how to make the most of it. What I really need is more help. My board of directors promised they'd try to get some volunteers together for a work day, but they're all in Albuquerque and we're stretched pretty thin right now when it comes to free labor."

Ry leaned against the wall, arms crossed over his chest, and looked around. "If we put in a good month's work, you could have at least the main part of the house ready by Thanksgiving. The downstairs renovations are going to take longer. There, you're basically starting from scratch."

Distracted by the possibility of being able to offer shelter to at least four women and their children in time for the holiday season, the *we* took a moment to register. "Ry, I can't ask you to do any more than you've already done. I'm sure you've got other things to do than work on my project. Besides, you told Cort and Laurel you weren't sticking around. I don't want to keep you in town any longer than you'd planned."

"You didn't ask—I volunteered. And I haven't made plans. I told Cort that because I didn't want to make him any promises."

"Don't you have a job you need to get back to?"

"Not at the moment," he said. "I made enough over the summer between the regular work and the freelance jobs to carry me until spring. Like I said, I'm looking at starting my own business. I've got some ideas I want to run by Grady—"

"Grady? Grady Beck?"

"Yeah, the old guy I was telling you about. You know him?"

"Um, sort of." Inwardly, Risa cringed. She should have guessed who it was when Ry first mentioned the local wilderness outfitter he knew. Grady Beck was another part of her past she'd rather forget. Her one run-in with him when she was fifteen had cost her an entire summer of community service.

Ry cocked a brow. "Is that all I get?"

"Let's just say I hope he doesn't remember me."

"I wouldn't count on it."

He pushed away from the wall, moved closer, and she let him cross the line from friendly distance into intimate space. If he'd been someone else, as big and physically daunting, he never would have gotten this far, never would have made it past the front door with her here alone. But despite the warnings of family and friends against trusting him, she felt more at ease with him than she'd ever felt with anyone and so there was no question of retreat.

She revised *at ease* to something very different when he began fingering the zipper tab of her hoodie. The slow rubbing motion was mesmerizing—more so the subtle shift of color in his eyes that seemed to reflect his change of mood.

"You'd be hard to forget," he said in a voice gone low and husky.

"Probably for all the wrong reasons," she returned. His proximity had stolen her ability to breathe and started her pulse thrumming.

His hand slid upward, tracing a line along her skin from the hollow of her throat to her nape, threading into her hair. "Never cared much for saints." Bending to her, he brushed his mouth against hers, the barest touch sending a tremble of longing through her. "I don't think you do, either. Maybe you should stop trying to be one."

Obviously he had never tried, because the way he tempted her, how he made her feel—made her *want*—was sin personified. Not bothering to put up a show of resistance that both of them knew would be a lie, she tugged him to her. Closing the infinitesimal gap between them, she turned the tables on him by kissing him, running her tongue over his lower lip to invite more than the simple brief touch they'd first shared.

As if he'd been waiting for her permission, or maybe her acknowledgment that this was inevitable, Ry pulled her into his arms and opened his mouth to hers. His kiss went from teasing promise to explicitly passionate so fast it dizzied her and at the same time swept her up in a surge of desire she couldn't have stopped even if she'd wanted to.

An urgency caught hold of her, echoed in him, and they tangled together, pushing at each other's clothes. He yanked down her zipper, the low growl of approval he made at discovering she wore nothing but a scrap of black lace underneath reverberating in her. She fumbled open the buttons on his shirt, and shoved it off his shoulders. She was made clumsy by his large hands shaping her waist, sliding up to palm her breasts.

His mouth ranged hot against her skin as she spread her hands against his chest and explored the hard muscle she'd fantasized about, reveling in his sharply drawn-in breath as she let her fingers slip lower to the edge of his jeans.

There was no thought to it, only pure, blind need, and it would have ended with them on the floor or against the wall, heedless of the stripped windows that gave any of the neighbors a clear view of them making love with passionate abandon.

Except Ry suddenly stilled, and after a moment, Risa realized the pounding she heard wasn't the thundering of blood in her ears but a determined banging on the front door.

She looked at him and he cursed, dropping his hands from her, letting her jerk her hoodie closed and hastily rezip it. Shoving her hands through mussed hair, she ran her tongue over her lips, tasting him there. He bit off a particularly foul word, sharply shook his head and turned away, leaving her to answer the incessant knocking.

Immediately, she wished she hadn't.

Del Garrett stood there, red-faced and mouth set in an indignant line, her hand raised to hit the door again.

Risa had no doubt from her expression that Jed's estranged wife had seen her and Ry through the front window. What Del was doing in this neighborhood in the first place was the question. Rumor had it Duran's showing up in Luna Hermosa and his revelation that he and Ry were Jed's sons had prompted Del to leave Jed several months ago. She'd gone to stay with her sister in Taos, only recently returning after Jed had the fall that put him in the hospital. She'd yet to move back to Rancho Pintada and was instead living with Josh and his wife.

"It's about time you answered," Del snapped before Risa could get a word in.

"Mrs. Garrett. I'm sorry, I wasn't expecting anyone." Risa caught herself twisting her ring and stopped.

"Well, that's obvious. I would think you'd have more sense than to stand in front of an open window doing—" she huffed "—and with *him*."

Del glared over Risa's shoulder to where Ry had moved up behind her. He hadn't bothered to rebutton his shirt and put a casual hand on Risa's waist, his steady, narrowed stare daring Del to take it any further.

"Jed must've told you I was in town," he said.

"*Everyone* has told me you're in town," Del threw back at him. "You just don't know all the trouble you've caused, you and your brother, showing up here, claimin' to be Jed's sons."

"Seems you haven't taken a good look at me," Ry drawled. "I'd say it's more than a claim."

If possible, Del flushed an even darker shade of crimson, the color change stark against the bottle blond of her hair. She snatched her eyes away from him, directing her ire at Risa. "It's just terrible what you're doin' here," she said, and Risa wasn't sure if she meant being caught with Ry or the shelter. Probably both. "My aunt lives right there." She stabbed a finger toward the house across the street. "I came to visit her today, and I saw you here and had to tell you how much this has upset her. Why, the poor thing is just plain worried sick about what kind of goings-on there'll be here once you start lettin' just anyone come and stay. Haven't you caused enough trouble?"

"I'm not here to cause trouble for anyone." Risa took a steadying breath as Ry's hand tightened fractionally against her waist. She didn't owe Del Garrett any explanations, and it would be useless to lay out her arguments in favor of the shelter and the women it would help. Del had made up her mind, like at least half the town, and nothing Risa could say would change it. "I'm sorry you see it that way."

"Sorry isn't good enough! You're the one who's goin'

to be sorry, you'll see. Both of you!" With a final resentful look that encompassed both Risa and Ry, Del flounced off across the street to her aunt's house.

Risa closed the door, releasing a long breath as she leaned her forehead against the hard wood. "I am so going to hell for the things I'm thinking about her."

"I don't think I helped your cause any."

Turning to him, Risa shook her hear. "Trust me, if you hadn't been here, Del would have still found some reason to give me a piece of her mind."

"Maybe I should have introduced her to Bear."

Risa laughed and felt some of her tension slide away. "You're not nice."

He shrugged, unrepentant. "Never claimed to be."

Suddenly Del's bluster didn't seem so serious. What did it matter whether or not she had Del Garrett's good opinion? She believed she was doing the right thing for battered women in the area who needed a safe haven and that mattered more than anyone's approval.

"We'd better get back to work," Ry said, starting to button up his shirt. "That list of yours isn't getting any shorter."

"I guess we'd better," Risa echoed.

With Del gone, the remembrance of what they'd been doing before they'd been interrupted came back into the room, bringing with it all the heady, powerful, turbulent feelings. Avoiding his eyes, she made a show of pulling the crumpled paper from her jeans pocket and studying the list of jobs, not really seeing any of it with her focus on appearing as nonchalant about their encounter as he seemed to be.

"Risa—"

She didn't look up. "Mmm?"

His footsteps sounded loud in the empty room, and in the next moment, he'd plucked the paper from her hand and slipped his fingers under her chin, lifting her gaze to his. "I'm not trying to pretend it didn't happen. But I don't know what to do about it." His touch became a caress, extending along the line of her jaw to her cheek. "I know what I want to do about it."

"I'm not—I don't know what you've heard or what you think." The distraction of him touching her was almost enough to make her not care. "But sex isn't a re-creational activity for me. And I don't sleep with someone just because they're—" She came to a full stop, feeling the heat rise in her face.

The corner of his mouth twitched. "Yeah?"

"Good looking," she finished lamely.

"What do you want me to say?" He dropped his hand from her face. "If I'm supposed to be confessing some earthshaking feeling, I can't do that. We both wanted it. It doesn't have to be any more complicated than that."

"I doubt it's ever been more complicated than that for you."

"You're right. I don't let it be."

"Congratulations. It must be nice not to care. Saves you a lot of trouble."

His expression darkened. She might have pushed him too far; she didn't care. His dismissing the connection between them as nothing more than lust resurrected old insecurities she'd never been able to completely banish: she wasn't good enough to deserve being cared for, much less loved.

It was stupid, because she hardly knew him, and he didn't owe her anything more than the honesty he'd already given. But it was her first instinct to retreat behind her long-standing defensive walls, to put up a show of defiance.

"It has," he said finally. "One thing I learned quick and early—nobody listens and nobody cares. If you want to do something, if you're going to survive, you've got to do it for yourself, by yourself."

As fast as it had come, her anger at him evaporated. In its place came a desire to touch him, not in passion but with comfort and tenderness. She wondered if anyone ever had, if he'd ever known love, ever been given the chance to love.

"You're wrong," she said softly. This time she reached out to him, gently cupping her hand against his jaw. "It isn't always that way. There are people who care."

His hand covered hers, and she thought he meant to pull hers away. Instead, he held her fast and pressed slightly closer to her warmth. "Maybe."

She felt like crying, for things lost and broken, damaged souls and missed chances for redemption, and everything he denied and she couldn't have. But she kept it inside, putting her arms around him and her cheek against his heart, holding him and being held, and letting that, for the short time it lasted, be enough.

Chapter Six

The call came when Ry was finishing the last of the breakfast cleanup and thinking about a quick dip in the river before he started into town. The barking ring sounded unnaturally loud in the morning stillness, startling birds and distracting Bear from his explorations along the shore. It half surprised him, too, since the cell service this far from town had been sketchy at best. Figuring the odds were it was one of his newly acquired relatives, Ry almost let it ring until the messaging service got it. But the noise irritated him enough to make him glance at the incoming number before he punched ignore and silently told whoever it was to leave him alone.

Seeing it was Risa changed his mind.

"Were you coming over today?" she asked.

"Is something wrong?" There was an underlying edginess that bothered him.

"We left it vague yesterday. If you had other plans, I was going to work on a couple of cleaning projects."

She sounded evasive and his nebulous apprehension began to take on the shape of real concern. "I'll be there in about an hour. You gonna be okay 'til then?"

"Sure, everything's fine. I just wanted to know if I could take advantage of you again today. I'll see you soon."

She cut the connection before he could press her further about what was going on with her this morning. They hadn't specifically set times when he'd help her out at the shelter, but he'd assumed, since he'd made the offer, they had some tacit agreement he'd put in at least a couple of hours a day there.

He wanted to get to her quickly, but he needed to get cleaned up first. So, stripping off his clothes, he headed down to the river. The chill of the water hit him hard, and he welcomed it, needing it to clear his thoughts and damp down the heat in his body that ignited every time he came within sight of her. This morning all it had taken was her voice, soft and a little husky.

I just wanted to know if I could take advantage of you again today.

Anytime, sweetheart.

He plunged under the cold water, resurfacing with a gasp at the icy combination of air and wet slicking his skin. Bad enough he couldn't control his body's reaction to her, she was messing with his head as well. She always seemed to be with him even though he hadn't touched her in three days, since they'd almost made love in the bare living room of the shelter.

Made love? Where had that come from? He'd never made love with anyone, just had sex. Making love involved feelings deeper than simple physical satisfaction. It had been a long time, if ever, that he'd believed in anything to do with love.

The problem was, he couldn't imagine himself having sex with Risa and it being nothing more.

Frustrated in more ways than one, with the cold no longer his ally, he moved back to the shore, quickly pulling on clean clothes and packing up what he needed for the day. Then he spent the whole of the drive to the shelter trying not to think about anything more complicated than the jobs he wanted to get done today.

Her car was missing when Ry pulled into the drive, but the front door was standing open. Uneasiness ratcheting up a notch, he roughed Bear behind the ears when the dog whuffled, bumping his head against Ry's arm.

Nothing stirred inside the house save for the drift of dust motes in the sunlight as Ry walked into the living room, Bear at his side. "Risa?" His voice echoed back at him.

A slam and thud from the back of the house had him striding fast in that direction. He hit the kitchen door just as Risa hauled another box from the back porch inside and dropped it on the floor.

She straightened quickly, slightly startled at his sudden entrance. "Ry—"

"Are you okay?" Not waiting for her answer, he took two steps to her side and looked her over.

"I'm fine. Why wouldn't I be?"

He shook his head. "Damned if I know. You sounded weird on the phone this morning. Then I get here and your car's gone. For a minute, I thought you were, too."

"I'm sorry. I was just trying to shuffle some boxes around. I didn't hear you pull up."

"That doesn't explain the car and the phone call."

Hesitating, she bit at her lower lip then sighed. "I'm

sorry about the phone call. I shouldn't have bothered you. I was just feeling a little shaken. Someone slit my tires last night." Every muscle in him tightened, and she hurriedly put a hand on his arm. "It's no big deal. It was probably kids looking to cause some trouble. I had the car towed, and Dad gave me a ride here. I'll have my car back in a couple of hours, so no worries."

"No worries. Right."

She pressed his arm a little harder. "Look, even if it wasn't kids, it wouldn't be the first time someone's been unhappy with me and decided to let me know it. I've had to deal with abusive husbands and boyfriends, and trust me—they can be a lot more frightening than flat tires. I can take care of myself." When he kept silent, afraid of what might come out of his mouth, she added, "Like I said, I'm sorry I bothered you with this. I don't usually rattle that easily. But lately I've been letting a lot of things get to me, and so, when I found the car this morning—" She shrugged, looking slightly embarrassed.

Struck by too many feelings at once, both familiar and alien, Ry seized on the most dominant one—the instinct to protect her—and pulled her into his arms, holding her carefully, trying to find a measure of gentleness in himself he could give to her.

"You didn't bother me," he said finally. "I wish you'd called me sooner."

"If I'd caught somebody in the act and needed someone to scare the heck out of them, I would have called you and Bear," she said. Hearing his name, Bear pushed against her leg, and, smiling, she broke their embrace to bend down and give him a pat. "I didn't think you'd be interested in seeing my four flat tires."

If he ever did find out who was responsible, he'd

take great pleasure in scaring the hell out of them. He didn't tell her that, though; she probably wouldn't thank him for it.

Straightening, she turned her smile to him, eyeing him with a questioning look before her face cleared. "You got your hair cut." She reached up and rifled her fingers through it before dragging them lightly over the smooth line of his jaw. "Better be careful, or you're going to end up looking all civilized."

"Looking, maybe. Don't count on acting."

If she knew what he was thinking and could feel how hard his body was for her right now, she'd know there was nothing civilized about him. To cover it, he stepped back and leaned against the counter, pretending it was business as usual. "You got your list? We'd better get started if we're going to get anything done this morning."

She didn't protest as they went to work. But over the next several hours, he sometimes caught her watching him, her eyes thoughtful.

It was late afternoon when, blowing out a long breath, she stowed the last of the paint cans and brushes away and put her hands to the small of her back, stretching. Her wince told him she'd had enough for one day.

"Ready for a break?" he asked, coming over from where he'd been finishing replacing a section of flooring.

"Definitely. You?"

"About two hours ago. Working inside isn't my favorite activity." Because he didn't want her apologizing for keeping him penned in, he preempted her by saying, "I was going to pay Grady a visit this afternoon. I haven't gotten up to his place yet. You wanna come?"

"You haven't gotten over to the ranch to see Duran,

either, have you?" Tossing the question out casually, she didn't look at him when she asked.

"I'll get to it, soon," he said, more tersely than he intended. He'd been putting it off for no good reason except—and he'd never admit it to her or anyone else— he found the idea of a one-on-one meeting with Duran, or any of his brothers, unsettling. He'd tackled mountains and whitewater, blizzards and deserts, and none of it seemed as overwhelming as accepting that, for the first time in his life, he had family.

He expected her to push the issue, but she surprised him by acting as if her question had never been asked. "I'm ready to go, if you are. I'm starting to feel a little claustrophobic myself."

Twenty minutes later, they were on the road into the mountains, their destination a spot by the river where Grady lived and based his business. Risa hadn't said much since they'd left the house, but now she twisted herself sideways in the seat to face his profile. "So, how long have you known Grady?"

"About ten years, I guess. I've done freelance work for him, off and on, mostly when he had big groups or he'd double-booked a weekend."

"It's kind of weird, when you think about it."

He glanced at her. "Me working for Grady?"

"You being this close to Luna Hermosa and Jed and never running into your family, or anyone noticing how much you look like your father."

"Not that weird. I've never been this close to Luna Hermosa. Grady's business is all over the Southwest. The trips I did for him weren't anywhere near here."

He wondered, though, as he maneuvered the Jeep along the winding mountain road, if things would have turned out differently if he had done any jobs in Jed Garrett's backyard. Would Jed have then been as receptive to acknowledging he had another son? Would his brothers have been as willing to bring him into the family fold?

Grady was waiting for them as Ry stopped the Jeep. He was sitting in a lawn chair under the awning of his trailer, the smoke from his cigarette hazing the air around him blue-gray. The trailer's better days had been about three decades ago; dirt and duct tape probably kept it standing. It was positioned on a small ridge overlooking the river and the two wood and tin-roofed sheds close to the shore. They housed an eclectic collection of canoes, rafts, tubes, kayaks, paddles and oars and other gear Grady used for his various river expeditions.

Crushing out his cigarette, Grady got to his feet, grasping Ry's hand in a firm grip. "'Bout damn time you got by here. I hear you and that wolf of yours been in town awhile now." He gave Risa a once-over. "Though I see how you got sidetracked."

"By a lot of things," Ry admitted. Grady, he thought, hadn't changed much over the years. Leaner and grayer, his skin weathered to leather by wind, river and sun, he still wore a long braid, a ragged bandana and the attitude you could take him as he was or leave him be, he didn't care which.

He started to introduce Risa, but Grady waved him off with a cackle of laughter. "She didn't tell you, did she? Wild little thing, this one was. She once hijacked a coupla my rafts and decided to take herself and her buddies on a little river trip. Busted 'em both up in a fight with some whitewater rapids. You were lucky it wasn't your heads."

"I was hoping you wouldn't remember," Risa said with a rueful smile.

"Girl that looks like you? Not likely. You've grown up a bit since then." This time his appraisal of her was longer and frankly appreciative, and the old man flashed a crooked grin at Ry. "This time I'd say it was the boy here who got lucky."

Distracting Grady from dangerous ground, Ry handed over the bottle of whiskey he'd brought, broadening Grady's smile.

Grady pointed them to empty chairs, with Bear sitting between them, while he went inside the trailer to fetch glasses. "Been a while since I had the good stuff," Grady commented as he sat back down to pour out the drinks and light up another cigarette. "Last time was a month or so ago, with your daddy."

Ry's hand froze in midgesture of reaching for his whiskey glass. "You knew?"

"Guessed. Hard not to, you lookin' just like him."

"You never said anything."

"Not my business to. When you first showed up for a job, you were already grown and doin' fine on your own. You didn't need anyone lookin' after you. I don't think you would've believed me anyways, or wanted to. And Jed ain't exactly the fatherly type. I doubt back then he would've wanted to hear he might have another boy. Now—" Grady shrugged "—him bein' sick and all, I guess it makes a difference to him."

Risa's gaze shifted between Grady and him. Ry could tell she wanted to say something, but there was wariness in her eyes. He should say something, but he couldn't decide how he felt. Anger had come first and quick that Grady had kept one helluva secret from him all these years. But he conceded the old man might have been right in thinking he wouldn't have believed it or cared enough to figure out if it was true.

It didn't completely erase his resentment, but it tempered it enough for him to keep his voice level when he asked, "How long have you known him?"

"Jed? Ah, we go back a long way. We was just kids when we started runnin' together. There was five of us then—me, Jed, Eddie Vargas, Anoki Viarrial and your daddy." He gestured at Risa with his glass. "Bunch a hellraisers, we were."

"*My* dad?" Risa shook her head. "I don't think so."

"Think again, girl! Joe wasn't no saint back then. If it hadn't been for Perla, no tellin' where he'd have ended up. Now there was a fine-lookin' woman, your mama. You remind me of her. Had all of us fallin' over each other to get her attention." He took a long drag, tilted his head back to send the smoke skyward. "But she wanted Joe, though Jed tried real hard to change her mind. He and Joe parted ways over that, and there was nothing friendly about it. Didn't matter much to Jed. He wanted something, he went after it, even if it was someone else's woman."

Ry and Risa stayed quiet, letting him talk, and Grady went on. "That's what happened with Anoki's wife, and why you got a brother that looks like he came straight out the Pinwa village. Anoki always thought that boy was his. Probably a good thing for Jed," he added with a short, harsh laugh. "Five women and seven sons. Always had his way with the ladies, did old Jed. No surprise to me he ended up with all you boys. The surprise would be if there weren't no more."

"I don't like surprises," Ry muttered. He reached

down to scratch Bear's head. "And I could definitely live without that one."

"I'll bet you could." Grady eyed him for a moment, then reached over to refill his glass before settling back in his chair. "What brings you out my way? Can't be a job. I'm not doin' enough work for one now that the summer crowd's done."

"That's what I wanted to talk to you about. Business." Briefly, Ry laid out his ideas for a partnership between him and Grady that would expand the business beyond the seasonal river trips and eventually, when Grady was ready to retire, have Ry buy out his share.

"I was wonderin' how long it'd take you to get tired of workin' for Billy Jackson," Grady said when he'd finished. "You're too good to be wastin' your time with him. You're too good to be wastin' your time with me, too, but at least you'd end up with the business down the road." Pausing, eyes narrowed, he asked, "You sure this is what you want?"

"That's why I'm here."

"Then I'm willin' to work it out. But when we do, that means you're based here. You thought about that? You like keepin' to yourself, but that might be kinda hard with that new family of yours practically livin' next door."

"I've thought about it," Ry admitted and knew Grady was right. "I'll deal with that when and if I have to. For now, I'm more interested in getting this settled between us."

There were a slew of details left over that were going to take time to sort out, but by the time he and Risa left Grady's place, Ry had a handshake deal with the old man to start the process of making their newly agreed-upon partnership a legal reality. Evening had settled in. Focused on going back over the meeting with Grady, Ry didn't notice he'd made the entire trip back into town without saying a word to Risa. That she seemed to understand and had left him to his thoughts intensified both his appreciation of her and his guilt at ignoring her.

He looked over at her, and she shook her head, smiling a little. "If you're going to apologize, don't. You've got a lot on your mind right now."

"I'm still sorry."

"Then buy me dinner, and I'll let you off the hook. I'm starving."

They settled on cheeseburgers at the local diner, pretended no one was watching and whispering behind their backs, and spent the time talking about the possibilities for Ry's new business venture and how long it would take him to put his plans for fall and winter expeditions into action.

"I like your ideas," Risa said as she pushed aside the remains of her dinner. "Especially the Telemark skiing and ice climbing. I'll bet you'll do well with those, once you get established."

"It might take a year or two. But we can make enough over the spring and summer to carry us through a few slow winters. And I can always pick up construction work if things get too tough. I've done it before. If you'll give me a good reference, that is," he added with a slight smile.

"Oh, I'm sure we can work something out." The mischief faded from her expression. "This all sounds good, but what Grady said, about you being based in Luna Hermosa—how do you really feel about it?"

"I'd rather not. But I won't get a better shot at my own business. This line of work, unless you inherit someone else's business, your chances of starting your own and having it succeed are next to nothing."

She nodded. "I wish Grady had told you about Jed. Maybe it would have changed things."

"How?"

"I don't know. The whole family thing might have been easier to accept if you'd known about Jed and your brothers before now."

"I doubt it. I'd given up on ever having a family long before I met Grady. Like he said, I'm used to being on my own." He picked up his beer bottle and leaned back in the booth, taking a long swallow. "Interesting, what Grady said about your dad."

Drawing patterns in the wet spot left by his bottle and her glass, she fixed her eyes there. "I still can't believe that."

"Why not? Look at you—you're different. I'm pretty sure you don't go around stealing rafts now." Smiling a little, she shook her head. "Risa…" She lifted her gaze to his. "People change. Whatever you did back then that you think can't be forgiven doesn't matter anymore."

He got no answer for that, but she suddenly looked away and he knew she didn't believe it.

By mutual silent agreement they left a few minutes later, and he took her back to the shelter so she could check to make sure things were locked up for the night. Her car was back, parked in the driveway with a note on the windshield from her dad, saying he'd picked it up for her earlier.

"Looks like I'm mobile again," she commented, balling up the note and tossing it on the front seat with her bag. She ran both hands through her hair, let them slide down to rest on the curve between her shoulders and neck. "I should get back to the house. It's going to be another early day tomorrow. Thanks for getting me out of here for a while. I really needed it."

"I'm glad you were there." He almost added he had really needed that, too. But it was something he had never said to anyone; he doubted he could even put it into words.

"Me, too. So…" She looked away, then back again. "See you tomorrow?"

He nodded, and she smiled.

Coming close, she put her hands on his shoulders, rose up on her toes and kissed him, a slow, sensual caress of her mouth that prompted his arms to wrap around her. He deepened their kiss before his brain caught up with his body's desires.

His body wasn't listening to his brain anyway, and he had no intention of pushing her away when he wanted her even closer. Her arms wound around his neck, one ankle hooked against his, as his hand tangled in her hair, the other low on her back.

Later, during many sleepless nights, he blamed himself and his lack of self-control around her for him not hearing the truck as it pulled up the street in front of the house, slowing down near the shelter.

But he heard nothing but his name on her breath and the roar of his own heartbeat in his head until the front window of the house shattered.

Chapter Seven

"You okay?" Ry sat across the kitchen table from Risa, fighting the urge to get her to a safe place then scour the town until he found the guys responsible. The police had left, and though she'd put on a brave facade for them, he could tell by the coffee mug trembling in her shaky grasp, the vandals had frightened her. He'd like to do a lot more than frighten them in return.

"I'm okay...fine." She stared at her coffee, avoiding his eyes. "It was only a few rocks and a BB gun, and the worst of it was a broken window. It was probably a bunch of teenagers with nothing better to do than cause me trouble. I'm sure their parents didn't discourage them, considering some of the comments I've gotten about the shelter."

"Maybe. I hope that's all it was."

"It won't last," she said, sounding as if she was trying

to convince herself. "After a while, once we're open, they'll give up."

"Probably. But in case they decide to come back before then, think I'll start camping out here."

Risa's chin jerked up, her dark eyes wide. "No, Ry, please, that's not necessary."

"Yeah, it is. We're just starting to get this place in shape. I'm not gonna let someone screw it up." Bending to the big dog at his side, Ry ruffled Bear's ears. "How's that sound, buddy? You oughta appreciate the warm bed."

"If it's a matter of you being more comfortable—"

"No, that's not it. At least for me. If whoever did this comes back, I want to be here."

"I don't know," she said, her expression troubled. "I'm not sure it's a good idea."

"I am." The corner of his mouth curled slightly. "Besides, if I'm here, you'll get more work out of me, and we'll get this place ready to open a lot faster. I don't have any jobs lined up at the moment so take advantage of it while you can."

"I guess I can't argue with that."

"Then it's done. I'll get my stuff tomorrow." Satisfied he'd convinced her, Ry got to his feet, offering her a hand up. She curled her fingers into his, and he used the advantage to gently tug her closer. He brushed back the hair slanting over her eyes and asked again, "You sure you're okay?"

"How could I not be?" she assured him. "I've got the best bodyguard in town."

"Then let's get you home."

"I can find my way home. I'm sure after all the excitement with the police showing up, whoever did this is miles away."

Ry pulled his keys from his pocket and whistled to Bear. "Got your keys?" he asked, moving to quickly double check all of the locks.

"You're not listening." She grabbed her purse from the table and fell in next to him.

"That's 'cause you haven't said much worth hearing."

"Ever the charmer, aren't you?"

With that he turned and pulled her against his chest to kiss her soundly. She matched his intensity, gripping his shoulders to mold her body to his, as if she needed the security of his embrace.

When they'd caught their breath a few minutes later, Ry took her hand to lead her outside, answering her with a slight smile, "I always did think charm was a waste of time."

The next couple of days of him staying at the shelter passed without incident. But all of the hours painting, repairing and laying new tile had given Ry too much time to think. His avoidance of Duran had begun to eat at his conscience, no longer refusing to yield to excuses.

Finally, alone while Risa tackled a list of errands, the hammering of guilt in his head grew louder than that of the tool in his hand. He jerked his cell phone out of his pocket, glowered at it a moment, then punched in Duran's number.

Duran picked up on the third ring. "Hey, it's Ry. You busy?"

"Just working on some editing. I don't start filming the new documentary until after the holidays. Is everything all right there?"

After word of the vandalism had gotten out, all Ry's brothers had offered to help, but Ry had managed to convince them that he had the situation covered. "It's good for now. I'm camping here for a while in case they come back."

"Be careful," Duran warned. "There are some people in town who aren't too happy with what Risa's trying to do there."

"They haven't met Bear."

"Good point. So what's up?"

"I was thinking of taking a break, and I—" He stopped, not sure what he wanted.

"You want to come by the ranch? Lia's going to be late getting home from the hospital," Duran said of his pediatrician's fiancé, "but Noah and I are here."

The enthusiasm in his brother's voice chafed him, but Ry forced back his irritation. "Okay, give me an hour or so."

Setting aside his current project, he used the time it took to clean up and drive to the ranch to mull over his meeting with Duran. This would be the first time they'd spent in each other's company since Duran had come looking for him to save Noah's life. Duran and Ry were twins—though there was little physical evidence to support that truth—but his brother might as well have been a stranger for all he knew about him.

If Duran's thoughts mirrored his, it didn't show as Duran let Ry into the ranch house and guided him back to the south wing, where he and Noah were temporarily living. "Good timing. Noah fell asleep a few minutes ago, and I'm finished with work for the day."

"How's he doing?" Ry asked.

"Really well. So much better than I'd ever dared to hope. Coming here was the best thing I ever did. Everyone's been great about making us part of the family, although having Lia in our lives has made the biggest difference."

"Yeah, I can imagine," Ry returned, though he couldn't. His brother's sense of family was so alien to him, finding the right response felt like more of a challenge than any he'd ever faced.

Grabbing a couple of beers, Duran led Ry out to the back patio. "Do you mind sitting outside? It's a little cool, but we can catch the last of the sun."

"You like the outdoors?" Somehow Ry had pictured his brother, the documentary filmmaker, as a video geek who rarely saw daylight.

"You sound surprised," Duran said, laughing a little. He settled into an oversized Mexican rattan chair across from Ry. "We are twins, after all. We've obviously gone in different directions, but I can't help but believe we've got some things in common."

"Don't see how that's possible."

Duran shrugged. "Genetics. Look at you and Jed."

Ry caught Duran's sideways glance in time to quell his instinct to take offense.

"Sorry, couldn't resist that one."

"Why should I expect you to? No one else does."

"So what do you think of him?"

Ry took a long drink of his beer. "Not much yet. Most of what I know about him is what I've been told."

"By our brothers?"

"Risa, mostly. The rest of 'em…" He suddenly needed to make some kind of connection with Duran to find out how he was dealing with strangers who were now family. Part of him obstinately resisted the impulse to talk to Duran as a brother; another part of him, newly discovered, compelled him to try. "How can you handle all of this? It's…suffocating, sometimes."

"I know it feels that way at first," Duran said. "It did to me, too."

Ry stiffened. "You don't have to say that. You're way more into family than I am. You grew up with one."

"That's true," Duran agreed. "But my family consisted of my parents and me. Believe me, when I first got here and all of them descended on me and Noah, I wanted to run. I might have, if it hadn't been for Noah."

Ry looked at the sincerity in his brother's eyes, and something deep down inside warmed. "I wouldn't have thought that."

The feeling lingered, and although it was foreign and strange, he found it wasn't unwelcome. It was a sense he wasn't alone in the world; the opposite of what he'd hardened himself to accept from his boyhood to this very moment.

"There might be a few other things you don't know about me and our brothers, and maybe even Jed." When Ry shot him a skeptical look, Duran amended, "Big maybe there, okay?"

"I'd say. Risa said he was tough and mean, and she didn't exaggerate."

"You must be talking about Jed," a voice called from the open doorway to the patio. Ry and Duran turned around.

Ry figured the beautiful redhead smiling at his brother must be Duran's fiancé, Lia Kerrigan. His opinion was confirmed when she walked over to Duran's side and Duran slid an arm around her.

"I didn't mean to interrupt," she said, looking between the two men. "I just wanted to let you know I was here."

"I'm glad you are. You haven't met Ry."

"It's nice to finally meet you," Lia said. "Duran's talked a lot about you."

Before Ry could think of a reply to that or to speculate on exactly what his brother had said, a boy with messy dark hair appeared in the doorway, hugging a scruffy stuffed panda and rubbing his eyes. "I didn't know where you were."

"Right here, buddy," Duran said. He held out his free arm, and the boy, who looked like a younger version of Duran, climbed onto his lap, positioning himself so he could lean against both his father and Lia. "Noah, this is your uncle Ry. He came to visit us today."

Noah, his mouth pursed, appraised Ry, leaving Ry feeling like he was being tested and wondering if he'd pass. Then the boy grinned. "Uncle Rafe said you have a really big dog that looks like a bear and that his name is Bear. Can I see him? I want a dog, but Mom and Dad said I have to wait until we find a house."

"Ah—I left him with a friend today," Ry said. "Maybe another time, okay?" It was hard not to like the kid, with his enthusiasm and his innocent acceptance of a stranger as part of his family. Here was one newfound family member, at least, who wasn't going to make comparisons between Ry and Jed, and question how much like the old man he was.

"I don't know about you," Lia said, brushing Noah's hair from his face, "but I'm hungry. You and Percy—" she tweaked the panda's ear "—want to help me make dinner?"

Noah nodded, then looked back at Ry. "Are you staying for dinner, Uncle Ry?"

Ry's throat tightened. The boy's invitation both

warmed and stung Ry. The last thing he'd ever imagined was one day he'd be some kid's uncle. "Thanks, but I need to get back," he answered in a voice he hoped was less gruff than his usual tone. "Risa's got Bear with her at the shelter," he added for Duran and Lia's benefit, "but I don't want to leave her there alone for too long."

"It's terrible, what happened with the broken window and someone cutting Risa's tires," Lia said, shaking her head. "Here she is trying to help women and children in need and someone does that."

"If it happens again," Ry said grimly, "I'll make sure it's the last time."

Lia and Duran exchanged a glance over Noah's head. "You'll have to stay for dinner next time, then," she said. "And tell Risa to call if there's anything we can do to help." She took Noah's hand. "Come on, you two. Let's see what we can rustle up in the kitchen."

"We mean it," Duran said a few minutes later as he walked Ry back to the Jeep. "We're here for you and Risa, whatever you need." He hesitated, then laid a hand on Ry's shoulder. "I'm glad you dropped by."

"Yeah, well, I figured it was time." Ry fumbled with the words. He was no good at expressing his feelings, especially when he didn't recognize them. "Thanks. For everything."

"Don't be a stranger, okay?"

Ry allowed himself a wry smile. "Little late for that. I doubt you'd let me, anyway."

But driving away from the ranch, thinking about it, he realized that, for the first time, the idea of acknowledging his twin, having a brother in his life, wasn't the unwanted burden he'd once believed it would be.

* * *

"Ouch, dang it!" Risa cursed, grabbing her lower back and rising from where she'd been hunched for over an hour scrubbing a stubbornly stained tub.

Sprawled half over the bathroom tiles next to her, Bear raised his ears suddenly and lumbered to his feet. His bulk nearly knocked Risa into the tub.

"Thanks, Bear. Are you suggesting I need a bath?"

"I'd guess you need dinner more."

Risa turned around at the familiar rumble of Ry's voice. He stood in the doorway, bending slightly to ruffle Bear's fur, and the sight of him quickened something inside her. It wasn't just that he looked totally hot, faded jeans hugging his thighs, his worn green fleece reflecting the color of his eyes and enhancing his rugged good looks. She admitted that even with Bear's protective presence, she'd been apprehensive working alone in the now darkened shelter house. With Ry there, the nervous tension in her eased, and she smiled. "You'd be right," she told him. "Are you making me an offer?"

"Now there's a loaded question."

Slowly, he looked her up and down, creating a different kind of tension, warm and seductive, that slid along her veins and tempted her to ask him to demonstrate what he had in mind. Instead she said, "I was hoping I could talk you into another cheeseburger at the diner."

"I can do that," he said, "as long as I get to pick dessert."

He took a step into the room and reached for her. The low sound of satisfaction he made deep in his throat as she enthusiastically returned his kiss chased away the last of her uneasiness and replaced it with desire.

"How about dessert first?" he murmured, busy

making a trail of open-mouthed kisses along her neck while his hands slid up under the edges of her sweater.

"I need food first," she said, though reluctant to stop him. "For energy, you know …."

His half smile and the glint in his eyes nearly made her take it back. "Better make that cheeseburger a double."

They walked into the diner holding hands, creating a ripple of interest among the patrons as they found their table. No sooner had they sat down and placed their orders, than a friend from the past, rounder at the middle but just as eternally cheerful as ever, made her way to Risa's side, hugging her as Risa stood up to greet her. "Long time, no see, girl. I heard from Maya you were home, but you've been hiding."

"Val, wow, it has been ages. You look great."

Val *tsked*. "You're lying, but I'll take it. I'd like to blame my brood over there for my full figure, but the truth is I can't stay away from the tamales and enchiladas."

Though Val was speaking to Risa, her eyes were riveted on Ry. Risa took the hint and reluctantly introduced him. "Val Ortiz, this is Ry Kincaid. Val's an old friend. Her husband, Paul, over there is a firefighter at the same station where Sawyer's a paramedic."

Cutting pieces of chicken for a boy who looked to be about five, Paul paused and lifted a hand in greeting. Beside him sat two pretty dark-haired preteen girls, nearly impossible to tell apart save for their different-colored sweatshirts.

Ry inclined his head at both Val and Paul but said nothing.

"I would never have guessed you and Duran are twins," Val said. "You and Jed, on the other hand—"

"Yeah," Ry drawled, "I've heard that. Every time I go out in public."

Before Risa could intercede, Val laughed. "I'll bet you have. Are you two here to stay? Maya told me about the shelter, Risa, so I guess you're home for good. What about you, Ry? Joining the ever-growing Garrett clan?"

Risa just stopped herself from rolling her eyes. Val hadn't changed a bit. She wasn't malicious about it, but her bottomless curiosity could be trying, and from his stony expression, in Ry's case annoying.

"Haven't decided yet," he answered shortly.

"Well, maybe you've got other reasons for staying in town," Val said with a sideways glance toward Risa.

"Ry's been doing most of the construction and repair work at the shelter," Risa interjected. "If it wasn't for him, I'd be looking at months before I'd be able to get it open."

"According to Del Garrett, you're moving along pretty quickly." Risa flushed, Ry's scowl deepened and Val, unrepentant, grinned at them both. She sobered just as quickly, turning to Risa. "I'm sorry about the trouble you've been having, though. But don't you let the naysayers run you off. There are plenty of us who think a shelter like yours is long overdue. I wish you'd been around during my first marriage. I guarantee back then I would have been the first to come knocking at your door. So if you need some help, I'd be happy to volunteer. Johnnie's in kindergarten now, so I've got time during the day."

Her sincerity touched Risa. "I might take you up on that, thanks."

They agreed to talk soon, and after Val said her goodbyes, Risa sat back down. "I'm sorry about all the questions," she said to Ry. "That's just Val. She means well, but she can't resist being nosy."

"Her and everybody else," Ry grumbled.

"Look, I don't like it any more than you do. All I can say is hopefully in a few months, they'll get tired of us and move on to the next scandal." He answered with a huffed breath. Risa poked at his forearm. "Weren't you the one who said I shouldn't give a damn what people thought? I think your exact phrase was 'screw 'em.'"

That drew a reluctant sideways quirk of his mouth. "Maybe I should take my own advice."

"Maybe you should." She quickly switched the subject. "How'd your visit with Duran go?"

"Better than I expected."

"Really?"

"Really," he repeated, sounding amused.

"You and he actually talked?"

"And I said more than two words. Some of 'em were even civil."

Risa laughed. "I'm impressed. You're making progress."

"Don't give me a gold star yet." He linked their hands and started rubbing circles over her skin with the pad of his thumb. "I could still mess this up. Probably will."

"That's okay. I'll still be impressed."

The waitress interrupted then, bringing their dinner, and with the atmosphere lightened, the rest of the time was spent in easy conversation. It was an hour later, as they were on their way out the door, that Risa found herself face-to-face with another part of her past.

"Risa?" A petite woman, far enough along in her pregnancy to be showing a gently rounded belly, stopped inside the doorway and stared. The man behind her put a hand to her waist, he, too, looking at Risa in mild surprise.

"Cat, I—how are you? And Rico—wow, it's been a while." Her own voice, stumbling over the words, mocked her. Catarina Ortiz had been her best friend since elementary school, until Risa had run away without telling Cat why or that she was leaving. And Rico Esteban... Risa wished in vain she could disappear.

"I heard you were back in town," Cat said, her voice shaded with bitterness. "But then I heard about that the same way I found out you'd left, from someone else."

"I should have called, I know. Things have just been complicated...."

"They always were with you. Apparently they still are." She flicked a look at Ry, who responded by taking Risa's hand.

Wanting to avoid being rude, Risa reluctantly introduced the couple to Ry. "I didn't know you two were married," she said.

"For almost five years now," Rico answered. He slipped a protective hand over his wife's belly. "If this little girl's on time, we'll be celebrating our anniversary about the time she's born."

Flashes of the past arose suddenly: everything she and Cat had shared growing up together; the time in high school she'd dated Rico, never imagining he and Cat would end up the happily married, expectant couple and she would be the one struggling to make a life alone, living down a past she was ashamed of.

"Congratulations. It's been great to see you both. We've got to run for now, but maybe we can catch up more later, Cat, okay?" With a hasty goodbye, Risa practically tugged Ry out of the diner and back to the Jeep.

It was a short, wordless drive to the shelter. Ry parked the Jeep behind her car and killed the engine, but made no move to get out. "Did I miss something back there?"

"It's just…nothing. It's nothing." The feelings dredged up by seeing Cat and Rico were too raw to expose to scrutiny, even knowing Ry wouldn't judge her. She didn't dare let her vulnerability show. She might reveal something she would forever regret.

"Yeah, okay." A long silence stretched between them. Then he said abruptly, "You want to come in for a while? I'll make you some coffee."

"I think I'll go on home," she said. "I'm tired, and the rest of the week doesn't get any easier. Thanks for dinner, though." Afraid looking at him would crumble her resolve, Risa hurriedly let herself out and made for her car.

She didn't make it three steps before Ry turned her around and held her fast. When he bent to kiss her, the sweet depth of it threatened her wavering control. But gently, before she broke, he released her, giving her a last look, and then got back into the Jeep.

She left him, but all the way home, in her rearview mirror, she watched the steady set of headlights behind and knew he was with her.

Chapter Eight

Risa sat on the front steps of the shelter, waiting for Ry. The late afternoon sun shone brilliantly, but she'd pulled on a woolly sweater against the bite in the air. Bear stretched out beside her, and she idly rubbed a hand through his rough fur, finding comfort in echoing one of Ry's familiar habits.

She'd seen more of his dog than she had of Ry in the last week. Since the night the vandals came, Ry had insisted on leaving Bear with her during the day and on following her home if she stayed past dark. He'd also kept his promise to stay at and work on the house, but largely when she wasn't there.

It was obvious he was trying to avoid her and she couldn't blame him. Their encounter with Cat and Rico had unsettled her and she'd been moody and withdrawn, unwilling to share the reasons with Ry. She felt bad for shutting him out, though, missing the closeness they'd developed, and she'd resolved today that she was going to talk to him.

Ry's Jeep pulled into view, and she stood up as he got out and slowly walked over to her. He didn't seem especially happy to find her there.

"I thought you might be gone already," he said, glancing at her then going down on his haunches to scratch Bear's head.

"I waited for you. I wanted to apologize," she hurried out before he could stop her. "I know I've been difficult to get along with lately. I shut you out, and I shouldn't have."

"You don't owe me anything," he said shortly.

"It's not about owing you. We're friends." The word sounded small and inadequate compared to the strong attraction and the bond between them. But she could think of nothing else to define them. "At least I hope we still are."

He didn't respond, kept his eyes on Bear, his fingers flexing on the dog's fur.

Risa silently cursed herself for letting her insecurities come between them. But she wasn't going to give up so easily. Reaching out, she touched his shoulder. He finally looked up. "Seeing Cat and Rico reminded me of things I'd rather forget," she tried to explain. "She's one of the people that I left behind. Rico, too—we dated in high school, and we were sleeping together for a little while. I never told either of them I was leaving or why I left. I hate that I hurt so many people. I'm still doing it."

"You didn't hurt me." He stood up, and for several long moments he looked at her, his mouth pulled to one side and a muscle twitching along his jaw as if he were working himself up to say something difficult. "I missed you," he said at last, his gruff delivery softened by the brush of his knuckles against her cheek.

"I missed you, too." She moved toward him at the same time he stepped closer and gathered her into his arms.

After a few minutes, he moved his hand to her face and slanted his mouth over hers, claiming an intimate, open-mouthed kiss. There was a touch of possession in it that intensified the electric, wanton need that sprung to life each time he touched her. She couldn't remember ever wanting any man like this, the strength of it overwhelming every other need and her common sense.

"Del's aunt is probably taking photos to prove her point about the illicit goings-on around here," she said, slightly breathless when they broke for air.

"Gives her something to do. Speaking of which…" He kissed her again, lightly this time. "I can't stay. It's not you," he added, apparently seeing the disappointment she tried to hide. "I said I'd go out to the ranch this evening. Jed's back, and the whole group of them decided it was a good time for a family reunion."

"And you agreed?"

"No. I said I'd be there." Scrubbing a hand over his face, he paced a few steps away. "I've gotten calls from all of them this week, and Sawyer and Cruz stopped by a couple of nights I was here. I finally said yes to get them off my back."

He looked like a man condemned to a miserable fate. Risa didn't know how to help, but determined to at least support him offered, "I could go with you."

"You don't want to be there any more than I do."

"No, but like you said about Aria's party, it might be easier if we walk in together. Or not," she amended quickly, thinking it could expose him to more speculation and questions. "I don't want to make things more difficult for you. And it's not like I was invited."

"You're invited if you're with me."

"Is that really what you want? Because I guarantee everyone there is going to assume we're..." The shift in his expression, his half smile, told her he knew exactly what she left unsaid.

He moved back to her, taking his time, his gaze roving over her body. "Anytime you want to make that more than an assumption..."

"Not today," she said with a lightness she didn't feel.

She expected some suggestive comeback from him or an attempt to change her mind. Instead, he traced his fingertips over her cheek, the caress almost tender. "I'd take you up on your offer. But showing up together might make things difficult for you, not me."

"Maybe." He cocked a brow, and she reluctantly admitted, "Okay, probably. But that's my problem, and I've got to learn to deal with it if I'm going to stay here. I can put up with it if my being there is a help to you."

"Why?" he asked and seemed genuinely baffled.

Because we're friends was the safe answer; she gave him the truth. "Because I care."

Ry stared at her, slightly frowning. Whether it was because someone caring about him was a new and untried concept, or because he was ill at ease with the idea, Risa couldn't tell from his reaction.

"I'm not asking you for anything," she said.

"I know. It's... No one's ever..." With a sharp shake of his head, he turned away and went to stand a few feet from her. Not looking at her, he fixed his eyes straight ahead and said in a low, tight voice, "You want to know the real reason why I don't want to go tonight? I'm a coward."

"Ry, that's not true."

"Yeah, it is. I've kept avoiding this because I didn't want to have to figure out what to do about all this *family* I suddenly have. I don't do that. I don't duck and run when things get tough."

"Taking on a family is different than taking on a mountain or a river. I didn't grow up like you did, and I'm still avoiding taking on mine. If anybody's a coward, it's me."

That had him twisting back to face her. They looked at each other for several moments, and then the corner of his mouth lifted. "Come with me. Anyone gives you grief, I'll tell 'em to go to hell. And you can interrupt anytime someone starts to ask me to dinner or another damned party."

"It sounds like a plan," she readily agreed. The idea of walking in uninvited to a gathering at the Garrett ranch should have made her uncomfortable and probably would, later. But Ry's willingness to go—and with her at his side—roused an old spirit of defiance in her, one that lent her the courage to face his family and her sister despite the questions and cautions she was sure to get.

She smiled at him, and he smiled back. Right then, the only thing that mattered was that they were together.

An hour into the gathering, Ry decided it could have been worse.

He'd caused a stir, walking in hand in hand with Risa. No one had commented directly on her being there, welcoming her along with him. But Sawyer, Cort and Cruz had each made attempts to get Ry alone, he suspected to quiz him about his relationship with her.

She'd been as stubborn as him, though, in resisting anyone separating them, and so far they'd succeeded.

"How are things going at the shelter?" Aria asked Risa.

They were all sitting in the great room, waiting for Josh and Eliana before starting dinner. Del was coming with them—from what Duran said, she and Jed had apparently been making an attempt to patch their marriage back together since he'd gotten out of the hospital two weeks ago—and Josh had called earlier to say they'd be late. The kids were scattered around, busy with various games, except for Cort's teenaged son, Tommy, who sat with the adults and kept glancing at the clock and the door.

"You had so much to finish, and the holidays are coming up fast. I know you wanted to be ready by Thanksgiving. But with all the work you had left to do, I don't see how."

"You'd be surprised. Ry's been there every day helping me with the renovations," Risa answered. "Another week or two and we'll be ready for the inspection."

Ry resisted the urge to glare as he became the focus of attention.

"It's really nice of you to spend so much time helping Risa," Rafe's wife, Jule, said, exchanging glances with the other wives.

The look was intercepted by Cruz, who shifted his sleeping infant son a little higher on his shoulder. "It would go faster with more than just you two. I'd be glad to come by a few evenings and give you a hand."

"I'm getting ready to start filming at the Pinwa village, but I could spare some time on the weekend," Duran added.

"We've got it under control," Ry said before Risa

could answer. "I've been getting some jobs lined up with Grady. But for now, I've got the time."

"You plan on staying around then?" Jed asked, gesturing to Ry with his cigar. "Grady says you and he got things worked out."

Reluctant to admit to his commitment to stay in New Mexico, but knowing he couldn't deny it, Ry nodded. "I won't get a better shot at having my own business. I'm going to start looking for a place here, once I wrap things up in Colorado."

"I'd like it to be my business you're joinin'," Jed said, yet with a satisfied nod at Ry's reply. "But Grady'll do right by you."

"You already got another rancher in the family," Rafe put in. "Tommy's gonna know as much as Josh and me in a couple of years." His praise drew Tommy's first smile of the evening.

"We're glad to hear you're staying," Sawyer said. "For a while there, we were afraid you were going to leave town before we got the chance to know each other."

The front-door chime sounded, announcing Josh and Eliana's arrival and sparing Ry the need to answer that one. They'd not only brought Del with them, but two more kids Ry didn't recognize. He guessed from the look of them they were Eliana's siblings. Tommy, though, had apparently expected the older girl, and the two of them, after awkward hellos, disappeared to another room. Ry did a mental review of the family tree, realizing that though the kids were cousins, there was no blood between them.

"Sammy wouldn't give us any peace until we brought him, too," Eliana said as the younger boy ran over to join Noah.

"You best keep an eye on Tommy," Josh teased as he greeted Cort. "Ellie's not too sure about her little sister and him bein' so close."

Eliana pushed his arm. "I didn't say any such thing. Anna's just a little young to have made up her mind that Tommy's the love of her life."

"And you figure one of you hitched to a wild boy in this family is enough?" Eliana shook her head at the laughter as Josh turned his attention to Risa and Ry at the back of the group.

"Hey, Risa," he said, coming up to them. "You must be hidin' out. I haven't seen you since you've been back in town."

"I've been busy," Risa said, smiling. "It's good to see you again, Josh."

Ry noticed the tension grip her, settling in her neck and shoulders, and the shuttered expression in her eyes. It reminded him of the night they'd run into her friends, the way she'd retreated into herself, and he wondered if Josh was someone else she'd left behind. He slipped his hand over hers, and she accepted his touch, curling her fingers into his.

Whatever their history, his brother seemed unaffected. "Same here," Josh said. He looked to Ry and stuck out a hand that Ry briefly grasped. "We've talked but haven't met. Glad you could make it tonight."

"'Bout time you showed up," Jed grunted from his chair.

"Well, we almost didn't," Del said. A small white poodle clutched in her arm, she pushed past Josh to confront Ry and Risa. Her glare swiveled between the two of them and then settled on Risa. "What are you doin' here? This is supposed to be a family dinner."

Ry shifted his hand around her waist, lightly clasping Risa closer to his side. "She's with me," he answered for her. "And I am family."

"You don't belong here," Del said, transferring her scowl to him. "Neither of you do. The two of you have caused us nothin' but trouble. I just don't see—"

"Oh, hush up woman," Jed said, cutting her off. "I'm not in the mood to listen to your mouth tonight."

Del flushed and for a moment, Ry thought she would continue her rant anyway. Instead, her mouth pursed tightly, she marched over to Jed. "This is all too much, all these people and noise. You should be restin'."

"Don't fuss at me, woman," he grumbled, but Ry noticed he didn't object when Del perched herself on the chair next to his.

"It's my fault we're late," Eliana apologized. "I wasn't feeling well earlier."

"I've got some tea that'll help," Maya offered. "I can vouch for it myself—it's almost a miracle cure."

"What, you know what's wrong with her just by looking?" Sawyer asked his wife. He stopped, took in Josh's wide grin and Eliana's blush, then shook his head. "You two going to share it with the rest of us?"

"In about six months, we're addin' to the family," Josh said, pride and pleasure evident. "We're gonna have a baby."

In the exclamations and congratulations that followed, Ry stayed back, glad for any distraction that took the focus off him and Risa. He looked at her, and when she noticed him watching, she smiled. The gesture was strained; a forced effort to make him believe she was fine that only convinced him she wasn't.

He didn't have a chance alone with her to ask what

was bothering her before dinner started. The meal was a casual, noisy family affair, marked by frequent laughter and a hubbub of conversation. It was about halfway through when Ry realized it wasn't as hard or burdensome as he'd expected. Instead, the close bonds between his brothers gave him a glimpse of what it might have been like for him if he and Duran had grown up together, with parents who'd loved them both.

That was why he'd come to Luna Hermosa, wasn't it? To satisfy his curiosity, the questions he'd had since he was a kid about what he was missing—what he'd missed. He didn't need it, didn't want those kinds of relationships in his life.

And yet, somewhere along the way he'd let dangerous longings creep in and infect his prized solitude. They were seductive, tempting the small vulnerable part of him to believe this was real and could last. At the same time, they conjured the claustrophobic edginess that had hit him at his first meeting with Jed.

"Ry?" Risa's fingers curving against his wrist brought him sharply back to the present. The rest of them were up, corralling the kids, making their way back to the great room. Risa's eyes spoke her concern. "Are you still with us?"

"Yeah, sorry. What're we doing?"

"You tell me."

They were the last ones left in the dining room. Risa stood up, waiting for him to decide. He got to his feet, seized by a strange reluctance to rejoin the group, still plagued by the feeling of not belonging.

"Let's go," he said abruptly. "Just leave."

"Now? Without telling anyone?"

"Easier that way."

"Yes, but you're the one who told me you didn't duck and run." She reached for his hand. "Prove it."

"Is this some kind of social-worker crap?" he asked on the way back to the great room.

"No, this is the being-your-friend version. You aren't going to decide what to do about your family if you avoid them. So say goodbye and then we'll leave."

He thought about it for a moment. "I'll do it your way, if you come back to the place I was camping with me. For a couple of hours," he added, to avoid giving her the idea he expected her to stay the night. "I need some peace and quiet, away from everybody."

"I'm not included with everybody?" she asked.

"No." Maybe it was too much to admit to her, to himself. But he'd be lying if he said being alone was still preferable to being with her. "So—we got a deal?"

She looked into his eyes, searching, and then she smiled. "Yes."

Getting out took longer than Ry liked. In the process of dodging invitations and attempts to nail him down on when he planned to make the permanent move to Luna Hermosa, Risa's sister managed to pull her aside. Ry, half listening to Cruz repeat his offer to help at the shelter, saw Aria put her hand on Risa's arm, her expression intent. Whatever Aria said had Risa shaking her head, frowning, before gesturing in his direction and walking away.

"What was that about?" he asked when they'd collected Bear, who'd been left behind to guard the shelter, and were in the Jeep, headed toward his camp. "Back there, with your sister."

"The usual," she said shortly. "Aria trying to take charge." Pushing both hands through her hair, she sighed. "I know she means well, but I'm getting tired of her warning me away from you. She's got Cruz, Cort, Sawyer and my dad doing it now, too. Apparently, since you look like Jed, you must be just like him."

"Well, you were probably lucky that he didn't know about you two until recently. In one way or another, he abandoned all his sons, and he physically abused Sawyer and Rafe. I don't think Jed Garrett's ever cared much about anyone or anything except his ranch."

She paused and Ry could feel her studying him, trying to gauge his reaction.

He wasn't sure of it himself. Anger against Jed flared, because there were no excuses for abuse. Stronger was the sudden memory that intruded—Risa accusing him of never allowing any of his relationships to mean anything.

It must be nice not to care.

And he heard Jed's voice echoing it.

I'd bet my ranch you've had more than your share of women you don't recall.

It seemed everyone thought—Risa included?—he was his father's son, uncaring of whom he hurt, incapable of loving anyone. They were all worried that because of his temperament, he'd inherited Jed's abusive traits.

"They're wrong," Risa said softly. "You're nothing like him."

"You don't know that."

"Yes." She laid her hand on his forearm. "I do."

He didn't contradict her until later, when they were at the river, sitting on a blanket by the fire he'd built. As if it were something they did every day, she leaned back against his chest, his legs on either side of hers, his arms around her, sheltering her from the cold.

"They're right," he said abruptly, breaking their peaceful silence with the harsh words. "I am like him."

"Ry—"

"I've never cared about anyone. I've never tried."

He expected her to refute him, but not to laugh softly. "I guess that's been some other guy putting in time at the shelter and following me home every night." She tilted her head and kissed the side of his neck. "Neither you nor anyone else is going to convince me you're even remotely like Jed Garrett."

"You aren't afraid I could be?" he asked, trying not to reveal her answer was important to him. She was his biggest defender, but if he believed she had the slightest fears about him, he'd disappear from her life as if he'd never been.

Her answer was quick and certain. "No, there's nothing to be afraid of."

Pillowing her head against his shoulder, she curled her fingers more firmly around his hands and looked up at the starry sky. "I know you'd never hurt me."

Ry's answer was to hold her tightly and, for the first time in his life, to pray that was true.

Chapter Nine

She held the envelope in both hands, anxious, yet not ready to open it.

"Go ahead," Ry urged. "Don't worry. Everything's up to code."

Risa nodded and tore open the letter from the city inspector's office, quickly scanning it. A wide smile took over her face, and, letter clutched in her fingers, she threw her arms around Ry's neck, kissing him in celebration. "We passed! Can you believe it?"

He spun her in his arms, laughing. "You doubted my skills?"

"Oh, no, I'm a definite believer in your skills."

"Yeah?" His eyes slid over her with a look as sensually potent as a caress. "Does that mean I pass inspection?" He kissed her.

This time she took her time, slow to slide her lips from his. "What do you think?"

"That maybe there's a few things I oughta demonstrate before you make up your mind."

"You really do want to give Del's aunt something to talk about," she said, tipping her head toward the front windows. She'd found drapes, but they were opened wide to let in the afternoon sun.

"Keeps her life interesting," Ry murmured right before he slanted his mouth over hers.

Between virtuously avoiding another mini-scandal and letting herself be seduced into sinning with Ry, there was no contest. He won every time.

They didn't get the opportunity to indulge each other more than a few minutes, though. The doorbell intruded, separating them, Ry with a short exasperated breath and Risa a frustrated sigh.

"I'm afraid to answer it," she said, heading for the door. "Things are going so well, my instinct is to think it can't possibly last."

She opened the door to a young woman barely past her teens. She was cradling a baby in her arms and had an overstuffed bag slung over one shoulder. "Can I help you?" Risa asked, careful to keep her voice calm and encouraging.

"Yeah…" The girl darted a look behind her, swallowed a sob. "Me and Patty need to hide. I heard this place was a shelter, like, for women and babies."

"We're not officially opened yet," Risa started. Then, at the girl's stricken expression, she said, "Why don't you come in, and we can talk? I'm Risa. What's your name?"

"Cassie. I—" Seeing Ry, her sentence broke, and with a gasp she came to a dead stop, her eyes wide.

"It's all right," Risa hastened to reassure her, glad Bear was in the backyard so the girl didn't have to face both Ry and Bear. "This is Ry." She went to Ry's side and curved her hand over his arm, wanting to show Cassie she had no reason to fear him. "You can trust him—he's a friend. He and I have been working together to get the shelter open."

Cassie looked between them, and her eyes flooded with tears. "Please, you have to help me. My boyfriend said he'd take care of us. He said he'd change. But look—" She lifted the baby's blanket to reveal bruises on the infant's leg and upper arm.

Risa felt the instant tautening of Ry's muscles, and she gripped his arm more tightly.

"Wayne did that," Cassie said, carefully tucking the blanket back around the baby. "He would've done worse if I hadn't taken Patty and run. When it was just me, it wasn't so bad. I mean, he'd get drunk and he'd hit me...." She shrugged it off. "But now I got Patty, and she can't get away from him. I gotta have a place to go. He'll come lookin' for me. Please..." Tears running down her face, the girl appealed to Risa and Ry. "Please help us."

In a precarious position, since she didn't have the permit to open, yet unable to turn the girl away, Risa went over to Cassie and, taking the bag and putting an arm around her shoulders, gently led her to a chair. "Cassie, do you or Patty need a doctor?" she asked, thinking of Lia Kerrigan, Duran's fiancé. "I know someone—"

"No! No doctors. And no cops, either. Wayne's dad is a cop, and if they know I'm here, Wayne'll know, too."

"We have to do something," Ry said in a low, tight voice that told Risa he'd like to give Wayne a taste of his own abuse.

He was right, but she didn't know what. Doing nothing wasn't an option; Risa remembered herself at sixteen all too well, scared, desperate and alone, knocking on the door of a shelter much like this one and finding a sanctuary. She couldn't do any less for Cassie, even if it meant breaking a few rules.

Over the girl's head, she met Ry's eyes, saw reflected there the same resolve to find a way to help the young mother and her child.

Patty started to fuss a little, and Cassie dug one-handedly into the bag, coming up with a bottle. The necessity of heating it gave Risa an opportunity to escape to the kitchen for a minute and think.

"Let me take care of that, and I'll also make you a cup of tea. I'll be right back," she told Cassie. She lightly touched Cassie's shoulder. "Don't worry. You're both safe now, and we'll find a way to keep you safe. I promise."

Ry had already retreated to the kitchen. His ability to be nearly invisible when the need called for it—not an easy task for a guy like him—touched her.

He stood with his back to the room, arms braced against the counter, hands clenched around the edge. "I don't know how you do this. I'd like to beat the hell out of that bastard," he ground out. "I'm sorry. I know that's not what you want to hear."

"Don't apologize. I feel the same way, every time." Coming up to him, she put her arms around him, sensing he needed the assurance of her touch. "But I have to focus on helping her. I can't send her off alone."

"I know," he said, releasing his grip to turn to her.

"She can't stay here, though. If I let her and someone found out, I'd risk never getting my permit, and that would defeat the whole purpose of starting this project to begin with." She shoved her hands through her hair, racking her brain for an answer. "If the whole damned town wasn't watching me, waiting for me to make a mistake, I'd go ahead and do it anyway."

Ry was silent for a moment. Then he asked, "What about your dad's? You said when I stayed there that he's got extra room. Could he put her up for a few days until we're legal?"

"There's that *we* again."

He looked away, then back, and a small smile almost touched his mouth. "Guess this place has grown on me."

"I'm not complaining. I kinda like having you around," she said, quickly kissing him. "And I like your idea. If you'll do me a favor and heat up some water so I can make tea and get this bottle warmed up, I'll call Dad. I'm sure he'll help."

When she'd confirmed that her dad was more than willing to shelter the girl and her baby, she moved quietly to the living room. There, she stopped midstride in surprise. Cassie was curled a little sideways in her chair, sipping a cup of tea, watching Ry as he held Patty, feeding the baby her bottle.

The sight of Ry Kincaid—big and tough, and determined to convince everyone around him he didn't care—gently nestling the tiny infant in the crook of his arm brought a rush of feelings that had Risa blinking back tears. She fiercely wished everyone who doubted him could see him now, because they would know, as she did, that he was so much more than the stoic face he showed to the world.

"I've found a safe place for you," Risa said, coming over to briefly touch Cassie's shoulder. She explained the situation with her dad, repeating again that Cassie and her baby would be protected there.

The girl's bottom lip quivered. "Really? We can go there?"

"Really. My dad's getting a room ready for you, and we'll take you there as soon as Patty's finished. He's taken in dozens of foster kids, and a lot of them had abusive parents. You and Patty will be safe there, I promise. And you can stay until we figure out something more permanent, okay?"

Cassie nodded, and Risa took a seat next to her while they waited for Patty, talking quietly to the girl about the long-term options she might consider for herself and her baby.

"I think she's ready to go back to her mama," Ry said about fifteen minutes later. He rose and carefully gave the baby back to Cassie. "Give me a few minutes to get Bear settled, and then we'll head out."

They waited, Risa leaning into Ry's chest on an overworn couch in her father's den until they were certain Cassie and her baby were sound asleep. When Risa tried unsuccessfully to stifle a yawn, Ry decided it was time to go. He could have left earlier, but he wouldn't have slept. Not until he knew the situation was under control and Risa was okay with it.

"Hey—you asleep yet?"

"No. Well…" She sighed, rubbing at her eyes. "Almost."

"She's gonna be okay."

"I know. But I remember how it was when I needed help and how much worse it is for women like Cassie, and I feel like I can't do enough."

"I don't see how you do the job if you take each one so personally."

Risa sat up, frowning. "Are you saying I didn't act professionally with her?"

"No, I'm not." This was coming out all wrong. Why was he even trying to communicate about a subject he was woefully unprepared to discuss? Nonetheless, something drove him to keep trying. "I thought you were great with her. It just seems it's a lot more than a job with you. I mean, when you were talking to her about her options, you sounded as if you were talking from experience, like it was personal."

Her eyes slid away to focus on her fingers, twisting at her ring. "It's my job to understand the challenges girls like her are facing."

Ry gave up. He was making things worse, and the last thing he wanted to do was upset her.

"Don't you have to be up early tomorrow?" she asked, still not quite meeting his eyes.

"Sounds like I'm getting booted."

"No, that's not it." With a sigh, she finally looked up. "I didn't want to keep you too late. It's a long drive to Colorado."

"Not that long." He was committing himself to staying in Luna Hermosa tomorrow by finishing moving the rest of his stuff from his old place to here. Even after he'd settled the business aspect with Grady, he'd put off breaking all his ties to Colorado, using the excuse of not having a place to live.

It had been Jed, surprisingly enough, who had fixed that one. Unknown to his family, Jed kept a cabin in the mountains not far from town. He'd offered it to Ry, saying he wasn't likely to ever use it again and there was no reason the place should sit empty. Ry had almost refused, having a pretty good idea of what Jed had used his secret hideaway for and not liking it. But Risa had convinced him it didn't matter and he probably wouldn't find a better solution.

Cruz had volunteered to drive with him to Colorado, help pack up and haul everything back. Ry could blame Risa for talking him into accepting his brother's assistance, too.

"Can you and Cruz get everything done in one day?" she asked. "I can take care of Bear while you're gone."

"Great. Thanks."

Ry gave a short laugh. "My place in Colorado consists of a couple of closet-sized rooms in the boathouse. I brought most of my stuff with me. But having Cruz and his Range Rover will make it so I can bring my kayak and raft down. We can easily do that in one day." Drawing her to him, he pressed a kiss to her hair. "It's been a long day. You should get some sleep."

"Thank you," she said. She slid her arms around his waist and laid her head on his chest.

"For what?"

"For helping me with Cassie. For suggesting I bring her here. I should have thought of it."

"You would have. I just helped you get to it a little faster."

She tilted her chin to look at him. "It was much more than that. You're a pretty terrific guy, you know that?"

"Careful, or I'll start to believe it," he said gruffly.

"I wish you would. Because I do."

Left without a response, Ry answered her in the only way he could. He bent to kiss her, small tender touches at first, but as she responded in kind, soon they were both momentarily lost in sweet pleasure, tasting, sharing, touching lips to lips, heart to heart.

He took the warmth of that with him when he at last left her, the scent of her on his skin, the taste of her mouth, but mostly the memory of her telling him she believed he was better than he was, even if no one else did.

Ry had slept most of the trip up to Colorado, partially from exhaustion, partially to avoid conversation. He knew he'd have to talk to Cruz some on the trip back, though. He tried not to dread it.

"That's it," he said with a final yank to the rope he and Cruz had tied to the raft and kayak now secured on the top of Cruz's Range Rover. The late morning Rocky Mountain air was cold and crisp. It wasn't quite noon, but they'd already stuffed the last of his gear into the back of the car. "I'll get the gas on the way back," he offered.

"Great. I'll get the green chili cheeseburgers."

They climbed into the Rover and Ry took one backward glance at the boathouse he'd called home for the past several years. It didn't go unnoticed by his brother. "Are you going to miss this place?"

Ry shrugged. "I had some good times here. Had a lot of fun adventures, like great whitewater runs with the other raft guides during the early spring melts and deep-powder Telemarking by moonlight." He lifted his shoulders and let them drop. "It's time to make a move, though."

"It's got to be hard to leave a place you were rooted in," Cruz said as he started the car and turned toward the open road.

Ry snorted. "I don't know what that means. I never stay anywhere long enough to get rooted."

"I can relate to that."

"You?" Ry asked, surprised.

"I grew up in about fifty different towns. I never stayed long enough in one of them to call it home. Until I came here and met Aria, that is."

"I guess I assumed you'd always lived in one place like the rest of 'em."

"No, my mom and I barely survived. She did the best she could, taking one odd job after another all over the Southwest, but it was hand to mouth. I was always the new kid in town, always the loner and the loser."

Ry tried to reconcile Cruz's description with the image of wealth and success his brother now presented. "I figured you for the kid born with the silver spoon in his mouth."

"Not hardly," Cruz said with a laugh. "My mother was a teenager who cleaned other people's houses, including the big house at the ranch. She and Jed ended up lovers, but Jed sent her packing as soon as he found out she was pregnant with me. He was set on marrying Teresa Morente—Cort and Sawyer's mom—and all that Morente money, and a bastard kid didn't fit in with his plans. My mother could have fought for more than she got, I guess, but she was young, humiliated and scared of big, bad Jed Garrett, so she ran instead."

"You must hate the bastard."

Cruz nodded. "I did. When I got here I wanted to kill him for what he'd done to my mom. But after I got to know him and my brothers, I guess I mellowed about the whole thing." He shifted gears and glanced at Ry. "Don't get me wrong. I'll never fully forgive him. But I have come to understand him better. And I've seen signs he's at least trying to make amends."

"Guess that's probably why he pushed this cabin on me. It's the closest he'll get to saying he might have some regrets about Duran and me."

"You're probably right. It's the same with him being determined we all get a share in the ranch when he's gone. We've got that worked out, I think, but we'll go over the whole thing with you and Duran after you settle in."

Settle in… A few months ago, Ry was sure he'd never get to that point, of being content to tie himself to one place. He stared out the window at the dramatic Colorado vistas rolling by. Towering, white-peaked rocky cliffs plunged into deep evergreen valleys. It was beautiful country, different from the high country in New Mexcio. But right now different felt right. Talking with a brother he'd never known existed, moving to a place with a woman he couldn't stop thinking about, a family he increasingly needed to know and understand—it was a change, but one that was beginning to sound like it might be for the good.

"It took me a long time to get used to the whole family thing," Cruz said, as if he'd read Ry's thoughts. "Sometimes I'm still not used to it, and I have to get away by myself. Especially when Jed says or does something that pisses me off."

"He seems good at that." Ry paused, wanting to bring something up but not sure if he should. *What the hell,* he decided, taking a first chance on actually connecting with one of his brothers. "At least you escaped the abuse."

"So, you know about that."

"Risa mentioned it. It bothers the hell out of me."

"Me, too. Sawyer and Rafe were the ones who got the brunt of it, Sawyer in particular. Seems like the old man had gotten it out of his system by the time Josh came along. That or Del put a stop to it."

"Risa made it sound like it was pretty bad."

"It was, from what I've found out. But Sawyer and Rafe have come to terms with it without killing the old man, so the rest of us deal with it the best we can." They sat in silence for a while, until Cruz turned onto the highway that would take them across the border into New Mexico. "Couple more hours. Are you hungry?"

"I can always eat," Ry said with a shrug. "Or we can wait until we get to town. Risa usually doesn't get around to eating until late, or she forgets all together. I could give her a ring, and she might join us."

"You two are quite the item these days."

"Yeah, so I hear," Ry said flatly, hoping to discourage his brother. Talking about Jed was one thing; he had no intention of getting into the subject of his relationship with Risa, especially when he knew Cruz's wife didn't approve.

"What's up with the shelter?" Cruz asked, seeming to take the hint. "I heard they caught the kids responsible for the broken windows."

"Yeah, at least that's one less thing for Risa to worry about. Fortunately, it was just silly, bored kids causing trouble. She's got enough on her plate, trying to staff the place and get the doors open. We already had one girl and a baby show up, wanting to move in."

"We? Sounds like you're in pretty deep."

Ry tried to read Cruz's expression, only caught a hint of concern. "Sounds like you object."

"I know it's not my business." Cruz waved him off. "I'm only asking because Aria's worried about her little sister."

"She's not the only one. Risa's getting it from all sides, you included."

"All I told her was to be sure of what she was getting

into. She said that was between you and her, nicely told me to butt out and I left it at that."

"So what's Aria's issue?" Ry asked, knowing he sounded defensive.

"She's protective of Risa. Risa's apparently had a bad time of it in the past, made a few mistakes when she was younger. Aria hopes this move back home will give Risa a new start."

"And I'm gonna mess that up?"

"I think Aria's worried Risa isn't ready to get seriously involved with anyone," Cruz said carefully. "She knows this shelter project is important to Risa, and she doesn't want Risa to lose sight of her goals again."

Ry put a clamp on his impulse to lash out in Risa's defense. Cruz was being honest. He was confiding in him, and a part of Ry was able to appreciate that despite his automatic urge to silence any criticism of Risa. "She's told me about her past."

"Really? All of it?"

"Yeah." It could have been a lie, he suspected it was, but he wasn't about to admit it to Cruz. "And as far as I'm concerned, none of it matters."

"She must trust you."

"We're friends."

"I can see that," Cruz said in a tone that suggested he thought friendship didn't fully cover it. "Aria might see it, too, but she's always going to be the big sister, so don't expect a round of applause from her when she sees the two of you together."

"I learned a long time ago not to expect anything from anybody."

Cruz didn't comment at once, but turned the Rover into the parking lot of a burger joint. "I'm starving. Let's eat." They were out of the Rover and on their way inside when he stopped Ry with a hand on his shoulder. "I hope we can change your mind about your expectations. You can believe me when I tell you it's okay to expect whatever you need or want from any of us. We're blood. Some of it's bad, but a lot of it's pretty damned good."

Ry forced himself to respond instead of withdraw. "I'll give it a try. That's all I can promise."

"That's good enough," Cruz said, and as they turned to go into the restaurant, Ry thought that, this time, it might be.

Chapter Ten

Finishing her adjustment of the large rug in front of the couch, Risa stepped back, eyed her work, then looked at Ry. "Okay?"

"Yeah, sure," he said, barely glancing at it, and when she laughed at his complete lack of enthusiasm, added, "It's a rug. If you want to get me excited, you're going to have to come up with something better than home decorating."

"What?" She lightly ran her palm up his chest to rest over his heart, teasing him with her smile. "You aren't going to give me any suggestions?"

His arm circled her waist as he moved them closer. "How many do you want?"

"As many as you have time and energy for."

"Sounds like a challenge. Fair warning…" Ry's voice dropped to the husky rumble that was almost as enticing as the stroke of his hand along the length of her back. "I climb mountains and ride whitewater for a living. Stamina isn't an issue."

"You seem pretty sure of yourself. But I'm not going to take your word for it," she countered. "I'll need proof."

"Whatever you want." With a glance around the cabin, he amended, "As long as it doesn't involve any more unpacking, cleaning or moving furniture. We gotta find something else to do together."

Risa couldn't argue with that. They'd spent the whole day getting the cabin cleaned up and organized. Cruz and Cort had helped Ry move in furniture and all Ry's gear, but she had come over early this morning to give him a hand banishing the dust and putting everything in its place. She'd felt free to devote the weekend to him after Cassie and Patty had left her father's house yesterday to move in with an aunt in Texas that Cassie's boyfriend didn't know about.

"At least you didn't have to repair anything," she said. Jed had kept the cabin in good shape despite it not having been used for months. The small rustic log house wasn't luxurious, but it was well-equipped, for the most part furnished, and comfortable, and the isolated mountain setting suited Ry. "And it's better than a tent."

"I guess. My spoiled dog seems to appreciate it." Ry nodded to where Bear was stretched out in front of the fireplace, warmed to sleep after his hours-long romp in the woods outside. "I gotta get with Grady to see about some better storage for all our gear. His excuses for sheds aren't going to cut it, and I don't have the room here. I've got that spare room packed to the ceiling as it is." With a brief look over her shoulder to the darkening vista of sky and trees outside the front window, he shifted his gaze to her again. "You need to get back?"

"Not really, but if you have something else to do…"

"This was it, and as far as I'm concerned, we're done. You want to grab some dinner? We can run back into town."

"How about just out to my car?" Risa suggested, flushing a little when he eyed her questioningly. "I thought you might want to stay here, after all the work, so I brought dinner with me. Nothing fancy, just tamales." She tried to quell the awkwardness that came with making the offer; she didn't want him to think she'd planned dinner as an excuse to linger, even if it was largely true.

"Sounds good," he said, neither his tone nor his expression hinting at his feelings.

He went with her to retrieve her supplies from the car and then helped her put together the simple meal. After eating in the kitchen, they moved back into the living room to sit by the fire. Ry stretched out in a corner of the couch, drawing her into his arms so she rested against his chest, her head on his shoulder. She kicked off her boots, curling up her legs on the cushions.

"So, does it feel more like home yet?" she asked.

"Home?" He said it as if unfamiliar with the word. "It's not that. But it's a good location for a base."

"It might be more some day."

"I don't make a habit of getting attached to any one place. I never know how long I'll be there."

She didn't pursue it further, because if she had her self-defenses, he had his, too.

She turned in his arms and curved her hand to his face. "I'll be here," she said softly and pressed her mouth to his before he could say anything back.

This kiss was slow and full of emotion that was deeper and more complex than passion alone. The feeling stayed, even as it interwove with desire, and it became something stronger: a need not just to satisfy a mutual lust, but to make love with him.

It struck her it would be a first for both of them. He had never let himself care enough for it to be anything other than sex; as a teenager, she had slept with boys as an act of defiance, proving to herself and everyone else she would never live up to her family's example and expectations.

But she wanted it to be more than that with Ry. She wanted to believe it could be more than that.

"Risa," he rasped against her ear, his hands roving over her shoulders, her back. "If you don't want this to go any further, then stop it now."

She pulled back enough to look him in the eyes. "I don't want to stop. But I want it to mean something. It never has, but I want it to with you." It was a risk, asking him to care, and it would reopen old scars that had never quite healed if he rejected her. She wouldn't compromise, though. Not this time. "If that's not what you want, then you stop it now."

The words hung in a long silence between them, and she waited, inwardly trembling, for him to decide whether the past was stronger than both of them.

What she wanted should have scared the hell out of him and had him backing off fast.

But Ry couldn't let her go.

It was that simple and that complicated.

If he held her, though, it would change him—*she* would change him—tempt him to believe that he was better than he was.

Frustrated at feelings he couldn't explain to himself, let alone her, he answered her by gathering her into his arms and kissing her. He tried, at first, to keep it a tender caress, to tell her with his touch things he'd never said to anyone. But she tangled her hands in his hair, opened her mouth under his and it was all he could do not to give in to what his body had wanted from the first time he'd laid eyes on her.

"Make love to me, Ry," she murmured in between kisses.

A wave of doubt hit him. Cupping her face in one hand, he rubbed his thumb over her cheek, her lips, focusing on the contrast of her soft skin against his roughened fingertips to avoid her eyes. "I'm not sure…I've never…" The half-voiced admission made him feel inadequate and slightly ashamed.

"Ry…" The way she said his name, with longing and wonder and tenderness, had him looking up. "I've never, either. I want you to be the first."

He didn't question why. Whatever he'd done to deserve her trust, he wasn't going to screw it up now. When she gently pushed herself away from him and stood up, holding out her hand to him, he took it and let her lead until they were in his bedroom, facing each other in the darkness.

"I need to see you," he said abruptly, and he didn't want the harsh glare of an electric light. He kissed her quickly. "I'll be right back."

Retrieving a lantern from the spare room, he lit it and brought it back to the bedroom, settling it on the bedside table so it cast a diffuse glow over the room. It illuminated her smile but also the flicker of uncertainty in her eyes.

He knew how she felt. They were both out of their element now.

It didn't matter. Maybe he didn't know all the subtleties of lovemaking, as opposed to mere sex, but he wanted his hands, his body on hers; he wanted to know how she tasted, how his name would sound on her lips when she came apart in his arms. He wanted, with a primal need, to make her his woman, completely and irrevocably.

More strongly, he needed to prove to her and to himself that he could care; that his parents, his past, didn't stop him from admitting Risa meant more to him than just a woman he wanted in his bed for a night or two.

Slowly, he kissed her and at the same time eased down the zipper of her hoodie, fisting the material in his hands and pushing it down until it hit the floor. Underneath was the same black lace that had taunted him in his fantasies ever since that first day at the shelter. He traced a fingertip around the edge of the lace, denying himself anything more because he feared once he put his hands on her, his control would be gone.

Risa shared his desire but not his hesitation. She unclasped her bra and slipped it off, looking up at him with an expression that was both invitation and plea. "I need you to touch me," she said in little more than a whisper. "I need to know that—"

"I want you? God, Risa, I can't think of anything else. I just want to make this…right for you."

"It is right," she promised as she stretched up to kiss him.

She bunched up his shirt, tugging at it until he stripped it off and tossed it behind him. Then he slid the remaining clothing from her body. For a moment, mesmerized by the sight of her wearing nothing but flickering light, he just stared, his only thought that at some point in his life he must have done something right, because even his fantasies paled compared to her.

"You're so damned…perfect," he said, and the last word was lost as he simultaneously claimed her mouth and lifted her off her feet to lay her in the middle of the bed.

Taking quick seconds to shed boots and socks, he joined her there.

Ry ran his hand over her body, the sudden catch in her breath echoed in his own, and for the first time— with her—he began to think of ways to draw out the pleasure and make it last a small forever.

She ached for him, was ready to demand, to beg, that he do more than tease her with the barest of touches and a kiss, when Ry started loving her in earnest.

His callused palm slid over her throat and shoulder to her breasts, caressing her at the same time his mouth moved hotly against her skin, as if he were determined to kiss and taste every inch of her. The sensations he created overwhelmed her with their intensity. Yet in the gentle, almost careful way he touched her, she sensed he was tempering his strength, keeping a tight leash on his control.

The memory of them both lost to desire that day at the shelter had her hands ranging over the muscles of his shoulders and back, and lower, over his hip, to brush over the hard outline of his arousal. Impatient with having his jeans between them, she groped for the button, but with a low laugh, he caught her hand.

"Not yet," he rumbled and then distracted her by running his tongue over her nipples before gently suckling her.

An electric need shot through her, tightening the

tension coiled low in her body. He shifted downward, and she gasped, arching upward, her fingers clutching in his hair as he stroked along her thighs, opening her to the most intimate of kisses and caresses.

Any thought vanished, and she could only feel. He brought her to the first peak and left her trembling, clinging to him as he moved up to kiss her.

She let him have his way for a few more moments. Then, with a quick motion that caught him off guard, she put her hands against his shoulders and used her weight to push him on his back.

"What are you doing?" he muttered, and it came out more of a groan when she started unfastening his jeans.

Taking his face in her hands, she brushed her mouth over his, looked into his eyes and said softly, "Making love to you."

At her urging, he stripped off his jeans and was compliant when she guided his hands over his head to grip the iron railings of the headboard. That he trusted her with his body and his heart touched her in a way that made her want to give him everything he'd ever been denied.

And so, starting with a kiss, she began loving him.

He was far from inexperienced, but with Risa it felt new, erasing the memories of every other time before and replacing them with her.

He'd never given anyone control in bed, never lost his own. But he'd willingly surrendered it to her, and now he was paying the price. Her mouth, her hands, her body on his were cracking his defenses to the point where he didn't know if he'd be able to rebuild them.

He didn't care.

When she brought him teetering at the edge, he

refused to fall without her. Unclenching his hands from the railing, he grasped her waist and moved her under him, covering her mouth with his before she could protest. She matched his urgency, wrapping herself around him and kissing him back as if she couldn't get close enough.

It was permission, an invitation to finish what they'd started, but looking at her in his arms, small and slender, dwarfed by his size and strength, he hesitated, afraid he couldn't give her the slow, tender loving she deserved.

"Ry…?"

"I don't want to hurt you," he said through gritted teeth.

She reached up, pulled his mouth to hers and kissed him long and deep. At the same time, she took him inside her.

His restraint shattered.

It was fierce and passionate, and, at the same time, it reached so far inside him that when she arched and shuddered and cried out his name, Ry knew he'd been right: she'd changed him because he'd let her into his heart and soul, and nothing would ever be the same.

He let it happen, welcomed it even, losing himself in her, until they were both spent and breathless. Resting his forehead against hers for a moment, he lightly traced his fingers over her face, memorizing the softness, her smile, the taste of her lips brushing his.

Although he was unsure if he wanted the answer, he asked her, "Are you okay?"

"Okay isn't how I'd describe it," she murmured, snuggling to his side as he shifted to his back and took her in his arms. "Perfect. Fantastic. Amazed." She punctuated each word with a kiss to his chest, the side of his neck. "And wondering…"

"Wondering?"

"Yes, wondering." She propped up against his shoulder, and there was mischief and laughter in her eyes. "Just how much stamina you really have."

The weight of doubt in his chest disappeared. With a grin, Ry rolled her on top of him and against her mouth said, "Let's find out."

Chapter Eleven

The first pale tints of the sunrise lighted the room when Ry woke with his face buried in a pillow that smelled like Risa. But his arm was flung over the empty space where she'd been. He pushed himself up, saw her clothes scattered on the floor, and the momentary tension that had gripped him relaxed.

She hadn't left him.

The thought had him out of bed and digging through one of the boxes he'd yet to unpack, until he found a pair of boxers. Pulling them on, he went in search of her and found her in the kitchen, looking very much at home. She wore one of his flannel shirts, the ends of it reaching past her knees, and she hummed to herself as she filled the coffee pot with water.

He came up behind her, wrapping an arm around her

waist, nuzzling her neck. With a pleased sound, she twisted around to meet him halfway for a long, slow kiss.

"Good morning," she murmured minutes later, her smile chasing away any doubts he might have had about whether she regretted spending the night with him.

"It is now. Didn't like waking up without you, though."

"I'm sorry, I needed coffee and—" her eyes teased him "—I figured you needed the rest."

Vivid memories of the three times they'd made love last night had him smiling back. With them came a feeling he didn't recognize at first. It was like contentment, satisfaction, only stronger, a warm current of emotion he finally identified as happiness. It had been so long—if ever—that he'd felt this good, he decided he could easily get addicted to having her in his life.

"Are you hungry?" she asked. "I managed to find enough supplies to make pancakes."

"Sure, fine," he said, distracted by the idle wandering of her fingers on his chest and abdomen that became more focused when she started toying with the waistband of his boxers.

"I hope you don't mind, but I fed Bear." She nodded to where the big dog was polishing off a dish of food. "He kept staring at me, and he looked so pitiful I couldn't stand it."

"Yeah, I don't fall for it anymore. But I guess he decided you were a soft touch. Maybe I should give it a try," he added. He slid his hand under the collar of her borrowed shirt, working free the first button.

"It won't work."

"No?" The second button gave way, and he pushed the material off her shoulder, bending to kiss the bared skin, his tongue tracing over her collarbone.

"Um, no…There's nothing pitiful about you. Besides, I'll feed you anyway."

With a flash of laughter in her eyes, she nimbly escaped his hold, turned back to the counter and started assembling the ingredients for the pancake batter. Amused by her attempt to get away. Ry closed the small distance between them and pressed his body against the length of hers.

"You aren't going to get any breakfast that way," she warned, but the breathy tone of her voice betrayed her.

He reached around her, plucked the spoon from her hand, spun her to face him and, the second before he claimed another kiss, demanded, "Define breakfast."

It was midmorning before they finally sat down to a very belated meal, and then only after several aborted attempts on Risa's part to cook ended with her banishing Ry to the opposite side of the kitchen.

She marveled at how right everything felt. It was so easy to be with Ry, without worries of being judged about her past or according to standards she could never live up to. That alone made him irresistible to her. That, and how one glance—a single touch—from him drove away propriety and sensibility and replaced them with reckless need.

They finished the cleanup, and Ry sat down, pulling her into his lap. "So what's the plan for today?" he asked. He'd thrown on jeans and a shirt, but she, not prepared for a weekend stay, kept his flannel shirt on while her own clothes were in the washer. She'd gotten no complaints from Ry. Even as he asked the question, his hand edged up under the shirt, sliding along her bare thigh.

"Oh, I don't know. Cleaning, unpacking, maybe some furniture moving. I mean…" His hand stroked higher, and she kissed his throat, nibbled along the line of his jaw. "It's not like we have anything better to do."

"Think not?"

"Remind me never to question your stamina again."

"Haven't heard you complain."

"You won't, either," she said, her vow muffled by her leaning in to press her mouth to his.

She was entertaining wicked thoughts of seducing him onto the kitchen table when an annoying ringing intruded. She'd tossed her purse on the kitchen counter last night, and now her cell phone was a guilty reminder that she'd completely forgotten to let her dad know where she was. She wasn't a child anymore, but she was temporarily living with her dad, and out of respect and courtesy she'd tried to give him a rough idea of her schedule.

"Ignore it," Ry muttered.

"I can't. I won't be long," she assured him as she slipped off his lap to retrieve her phone.

"Risa? Are you all right?" Her dad's worried voice sounded in her ear.

"I'm sorry, I should have called." She hesitated, fidgeting with her ring.

"I don't expect you to report in. But you said you were going to help Ry move in yesterday, and I wondered…"

"Everything's fine," Risa said. She knew where her dad was going with this, and she didn't want to get into another debate about her relationship with Ry. Not this morning. "My plans changed. I'll be back later this weekend."

There was a pause. Then her father said, "All right, we'll see you then."

Risa let go a long breath as she cut the connection. Dropping the phone back into her purse, she briefly closed her eyes, rubbing at her forehead. Behind her, she heard the scrape of Ry's chair and then felt his hands slip under her borrowed shirt, gently massaging the tightened muscles on her shoulders and neck.

"You okay?"

"I need to move out. This isn't working, me living with my dad again."

"Is that all of it?"

"No, but it's making things worse. I just wish…" Sighing, she lightly pushed against his hands, liking the callused warmth and the rhythmic motion on her skin. "I wish things between my family and me weren't so hard. It's mostly my fault—I'm the one who decided I could never measure up to them. I'm the one who ran away and abandoned everyone."

Ry turned her to face him and looked her straight in the eyes. "Maybe if you told them why, you could get past this."

"I think that's supposed to be my line," she said with a small smile.

"I'm the last person to give advice, especially when it comes to family," he said. "But it seems important to you to fix it."

"It is. But—it would be hard to tell my dad." In a restless gesture, she rubbed her hands over his, seeking comfort. "He'd be even more disappointed in me."

"I doubt that."

She shook her head, and he didn't press. Instead, he took her hand and led her into the living room. She curled up on the couch, watching as he stoked the fire. He joined her there and wrapped her in his embrace, simply holding her and silently offering her his support and comfort, both of them quiet for a long time.

"You can tell me," Ry finally said, his voice low and gruff.

She wanted to, yet she was uneasy about his reaction, had been ever since he'd told her about his experiences with adoption and foster care after his mother had abandoned him and Duran.

But not telling him might damage their newfound closeness. So she shifted to face him, determined to look at him when she admitted the worst of her sins. "I told you I was pretty wild and rebellious when I was a teenager. I started having sex when I was fourteen. It was stupid, and for a while I was lucky all I got from it was a reputation. It didn't last. Two weeks after I turned sixteen, I found out I was pregnant."

His expression went blank. He stared at her, and she guessed she'd caught him unprepared.

"That's why I ran away. I couldn't tell anyone what kind of mistake I'd made. I was scared and messed up, and I just—ran."

Ry scrubbed a hand over his face, breaking their locked gazes to look toward the fire. "What happened to the baby?"

"I gave him up for adoption." He didn't turn back to her, and she added, hearing herself sound more defensive than she would have liked, "I was sixteen and alone. I didn't know anything about being a parent. I couldn't even take care of myself. I figured the adoption was the best thing for both him and me."

"What about the father?"

Staring down at her hands, she twisted her ring, regrets at having revealed the darkest times of her past to Ry coming hard and fast. "I never told him. He wouldn't have wanted a baby, and telling him would have just made it worse."

A weighted silence settled between them—him stiff and staring straight ahead; her fighting tears over the memories and the certainty she'd broken something between her and Ry—until it stretched to the point when Risa couldn't take it anymore. "Ry—"

"It's okay," he interrupted. Her voice seemed to jolt him out of his brooding, and he looked at her again, searching her face before gathering her to him. "It's okay," he repeated.

If it sounded more of an assurance for him than her, she didn't care. She hugged close to him, and when his mouth sought hers, she returned the kiss with equal passion, wishing that all it took was desire to wipe away the shadows of the past that had come between them.

Hours later, while she lay dozing beside him, her head resting on his shoulder, Ry stared at the ceiling, trying to process the feelings Risa's admission had evoked.

He wasn't sure what he'd expected, but it hadn't been that she'd given up a child, her son. His head understood, but that part of him that hadn't reconciled with the mother who had abandoned him said Risa hadn't been much different.

It bothered him, too, that—like his own mother—she'd never told the father about his child. He briefly wondered if the guy still lived in Luna Hermosa and thought of her friend's husband, Rico, and how uncomfortable Risa had been running into the couple.

He cut short his speculation before it could go further. It wasn't his business. She trusted him not to judge her. She'd accepted him and his past; he couldn't do any less for her.

Her touch on his cheek brought him out of his thoughts. Awake and slightly frowning, she was looking at him.

"Is something wrong?"

"No," he assured her, but not without a prick of conscience. "Just thinking."

For a moment, he thought she'd argue with him. But she let it go and stretched a little, settling back next to him. "I could stay here all day."

"Oh, yeah? You think we'd survive it?"

"Maybe not," she said with a smile, "but I'd be willing to try. I can't remember ever feeling this good."

"Me, either." He moved them so she was half underneath him and he could see into her eyes. There were things he wanted to say, should say to her. But he'd never been good with words, and instead he kissed her and held her to him.

He didn't want to lose her. But the word *mistake*—the term she'd used to describe her child—hunched in a dark corner of his mind and created doubts out of the questions he had and uncertainties he couldn't easily ignore.

Chapter Twelve

A cold December wind rattled the old casement windows of the shelter. Risa looked up from her computer and added insulated windows to the wish list she was compiling. A few churches in town, some with members who'd become residents at the shelter, had agreed to launch Christmas fund-raising campaigns to help Risa complete renovations and finish the basement beyond the office she'd set up there with a couple more bedrooms and a bath.

So far things were going pretty well. Her upstairs bedrooms were now occupied with family groupings, women and their children seeking refuge from unbearable circumstances. And the waiting list was long. Thanks to Cort, police patrolled the shelter regularly. Cort's connections with the city police and sheriff's departments had allowed him to pull in payment for debts his former colleagues owed him, and there'd been no repeat of the vandalism.

"Hey, you, it's Saturday." The familiar deep voice filled the doorway to her office. "Where's your hat and gloves?"

"Oh, my gosh, I spaced out. We're supposed to go sledding, aren't we?"

Ry nodded, with a small smile for her forgetfulness. He looked adorably sexy in his stocking cap, snug green sweater and funky gray snowboarding pants. "While you get everybody ready to go, I'm gonna move your sleds to the van."

"I have sleds?"

"Hard to go sledding without them. They're a donation from Cort and Sawyer. Now that some of their kids are older, I agreed to trade ski lessons for old sleds."

"That was nice of you." She logged off and went over to him and into his arms. He kissed her sweetly and held her close, but Risa sensed a restraint in him.

Something had changed recently. She was sure her confession about the baby had prompted it, created a barrier between them. Neither of them had brought up the subject again, but she suspected Ry was wrestling with conflicting emotions, wanting to support her yet unable to separate her past choices from his past experiences.

Ignoring it and hoping he'd eventually come to terms with it probably wasn't the best option. But she didn't know how to approach him without making it worse. Unaccustomed to sharing his feelings, he wasn't going to bring it up first and was retreating behind his walls, using his old familiar method of detachment to avoid confronting his emotions. That left them at an impasse, one she didn't like and found hurtful.

It haunted her even as she made the rounds upstairs,

checking to make sure mothers and children were dressed in warm winter clothes, had hats and gloves and a change of clothes for the drive home.

With everyone hustling to get ready, Risa popped into the kitchen to give a few last instructions before leaving. "Bev," she asked the girl she'd hired to cook, "while we're gone, can you please run to the store and get some cocoa, graham crackers, marshmallows and chocolate bars for s'mores?"

"Sure," Bev said, looking up from where she was stirring a delicious-smelling chicken-noodle soup. "We're about out of coffee and milk, too, so I'll pick some up."

"Great. The kids will have a treat when we get back from sledding."

Satisfied with her arrangements, Risa went back into the living room. Ry was there, kneeling in front of a small, shy boy who'd arrived yesterday, wrestling with the stubborn zipper on the boy's parka. The boy solemnly watched, listening intently, while Ry told him a story about the first time he'd gotten on a sled.

It wasn't the first time she'd seen Ry's gentler side. She remembered him holding Cassie's baby and wondered if he saw himself in these children, kids who'd also suffered abandonment and abuse. Wondered, too, if part of him despised her for choosing to give up her own son, never knowing if the boy had ended up in a loving home or, like him, lost and unwanted.

"Got it," Ry said. Tugging on the boy's hat, he smiled. "Now you're ready." As he stood up, he saw Risa and asked, "How about you? You ready to go?"

Bear let out an excited woof, answering for her, and she laughed, dark musings chased away by the kids' happy chatter and calls of "Yeah! Let's go!"

The three mothers had met Ry and seemed to feel safe with him. When Risa proposed the outing, they'd all agreed to let Ry and her take them and their kids. One particularly fragile woman said she was scared of the cold and didn't like heights, but somehow Ry had coaxed her to give it a try. She still looked a little frightened, but holding her two kids' hands, she followed the group into the old van Risa had bought at a huge discount for a few thousand dollars.

As the van rumbled up the winding mountain road to a favorite sledding spot near the Taos Valley ski area, Ry and Risa led the group in a variety of silly songs.

After a rousing chorus of "Let's go Fly a Kite," Risa teased, "I never would have guessed you're one for road-trip sing-alongs."

"When you've crisscrossed this country as many times as I have, you'll listen to and sing about anything," he said.

"I guess all the traveling you do for work gives you a good excuse to get away."

A slight frown crossed his face. "It's work, not an excuse. And if you're asking whether I need a reason to get away, I don't."

"I didn't mean now. I meant from…" Me? Your feelings? "Everything else."

"Risa…" He reached over and took her hand and didn't pretend to misunderstand. "I said it was okay."

"Is it?"

"I've just got a lot on my mind right now."

She doubted it was okay but didn't get a chance to argue. A little voice queried "Are we there yet?" at the same time the hand that accompanied it tugged at Risa's jacket.

"Almost, sweetie. Only a few more minutes, right, Ry?"

"Less than five. The big hill's after this next pass."

Squeals of excitement pierced adult ears, and the moms did their best to calm their squirming children.

The mountain was alive with noisy, rowdy kids of all ages, but Risa knew the fragile women in her care might easily be overwhelmed with so much activity. "Can we get a little farther away from all these people?" she asked Ry. "These women have been through so much lately, I think this crowd may be threatening for them."

"Sure," he readily agreed. "Besides, some of these kids are pretty young. Best we get out of range of the snowboarders."

They found a quieter part of the hill and unloaded the sleds. Ry knelt down beside the boy whose zipper he'd fixed. "Gustavo—that's your name, right?"

Gustavo—barely as big as his name—nodded, bouncing the mop of overlong black curls sticking out from under his stocking cap.

"Wanna ride on a sled with me?"

Gustavo looked around Ry at the waiting sled. He turned and lifted his chin to peer up questioningly at his mom, Dolores.

"It's okay, *mi hijo*," she assured him. *"Usted será seguro con el hombre grande."*

Risa tried not to laugh, fearing for a moment Gustavo had a reason to be afraid of big men, but when his mother laughed first, she relaxed and gave in to the humor of the situation.

"What?" Ry glanced from woman to woman.

"She told Gustavo it was okay to ride with the big man," Risa said, unable to contain her laughter. "You don't realize how you look to someone so small."

"I've got a pretty good idea. That's why I'm soaking my knees in snow."

"That is very kind of you," Dolores said. She bent in front of her confused son and spoke to him in Spanish. After a long moment, lots of hard stares at Ry, a few glances down the hill and at the other sledders, the boy finally nodded to Ry.

"All right, then," Ry said, "here's what we're gonna do."

Risa and Dolores stood by watching as Ry patiently explained everything that would happen and how it would feel to sled down the hill, reassuring the timid child he would have fun and be safe.

His mother, grinning ear to ear, leaned toward Risa, nudging her slightly. "See what a good father he will be. I wish I had married one like him instead of an evil one like Rael. Do you two have any children yet?"

Risa started. "Who? Ry and me?" The woman nodded. "We're not married. We're just friends." Friends, allies, lovers—she could wish for everything else, but doubted, after her revelations, Ry wanted it.

"Really? I would have guessed you two are much more. The way he looks at you…"

Whether it was self-defense or professionalism kicking in, Risa abruptly curbed the direction of the conversation. She was there to help these women, not vice versa. "Look, they're off!"

The group watched Ry and Gustavo, masters of the hill, sway, slide and zoom down to the bottom. When they came to stop, Gustavo jumped off and waved his arms wildly toward his mom to a rousing chorus of whoops and hollers and pleas to be next to ride with Ry. Seeming to enjoy the rides at least as much as the kids, Ry gave each child several turns on various sleds.

"I'm wondering who the kid is here," Sarah, another mother, commented.

Me, too, Risa thought but had to smile seeing the grin on Ry's face each time he and his young friends landed safely at the bottom of the hill, and hearing him laugh as he high-fived his sledding partner.

She'd never seen him like this, relaxed and carefree. Maybe that's why he'd chosen the career he had. Rafting, skiing, he could play, have fun, do the things his childhood had deprived him of.

"He's wonderful with the kids," Sarah added. She turned suddenly to Risa. "Thank you. Both of you. This means so much—" She broke off, tears welling in her eyes.

Dolores moved closer and put an arm around the other woman. "We never get to do things like this. Our kids don't know what it is to be kids."

"I understand," Risa said. "We're going to do things like this more often, I promise. It's part of getting stronger, you and your kids, and learning how not to be afraid."

The third woman, Wendy, the one who'd been fearful of leaving the safe haven of the shelter, had her arms wrapped around herself. "It's hard not to be afraid when you can't forget… The past is always there. Like somebody watching you." Her shoulders jerked slightly, and she focused her gaze on her children.

Risa could empathize only too well. It echoed her own sense that all these years she'd been living in the shadows of her mistakes, afraid to step into the light and expose her sins and her failures.

With Ry, she had begun to hope she could finally lay her ghosts to rest. But his reaction to her confidences had shaken her fledgling belief, leaving her like Wendy, wondering if the past would always be there.

That evening, after much hot cocoa was drunk and too many s'mores were eaten, the night staff arrived. Risa, Ry and Bev had just finished cleaning up the last of the mugs and marshmallows and thrown one more load of wet jeans in the washer. Risa gave instructions to the two staff members and checked the locks. Then she and Ry headed for their cars, Bear following at Ry's heels.

Bear hopped into the Jeep while Ry and Risa stood beneath a sliver of a moon and a gentle dusting of falling snowflakes.

"I don't even know how to begin to thank you. You were amazing with the kids and the moms. You even got Dolores to make a run down the hill."

"I had more fun than they did."

"I'm tempted to believe you. You're a natural with the kids."

"They make it easy. They already know how to have a good time." Risa laughed a little, and Ry reached for her. "How about you? Did you have fun?"

She snuggled into his arms, the tension gripping her nerves easing somewhat. "It was a good day. This is exactly what I hoped to accomplish with this place."

"You should be proud of yourself for what you've done so far. I am."

"Thanks, but I don't think I deserve any accolades yet. We're just getting started, and I guarantee there are some rocky patches ahead."

"You'll make the shelter a success," Ry said. He shifted a little, and she got the impression he'd entered new territory he wasn't at all comfortable in. "I wouldn't complain if you'd let me be a part of that."

"I'd like that a lot," she said, aware that while that was true, other truths, for better or worse, had yet to be uncovered.

Chapter Thirteen

Risa finished checking the last page of the grant application she'd been working on for the past three days, hit the print button and stood up to stretch her back while she waited for the pages. It was the third application she'd done this week in hopes of getting additional funding for the shelter, and she was glad it would be the last for a while. Paperwork wasn't her favorite activity. The only benefit to it this time was it had provided her with a distraction from missing Ry. He'd been gone nearly a week, working back-to-back ski trips, and she hadn't realized how accustomed she'd gotten to having him in her life until he was gone.

But dwelling on his absence wasn't going to bring him home any faster. She was thinking of going upstairs in search of coffee when the sound of someone coming down the basement stairs turned her to the office door in expectation it was one of the women.

Instead, it was Cat. "I hope I'm not interrupting anything," she said. She looked hesitant, uncertain of Risa's reaction.

And that's my fault, Risa thought, remembering their terse meeting at the diner. "No, it's fine, I was just getting ready to take a break. Come in and have a seat. Do you want some coffee or tea?"

"No, thanks," Cat said, shedding her coat and settling onto one end of the couch in Risa's office. "I want to talk."

"Cat, about that night at the diner, I'm sorry. It was a bad day, and coming home has been...awkward."

"Is that why you've been avoiding everyone?"

"I haven't been—" Cat raised a brow, and Risa relented. "Okay, I have. I didn't leave on the best terms, and no one's forgotten it. It hasn't been easy."

"You haven't made it easy, back then or now."

Wincing at the accusation, Risa nodded. "I know." She made herself meet Cat's eyes. "I know I hurt you. I hurt a lot of people. But I'd messed up so many things. I couldn't tell anybody, and I didn't know how to fix them, so I ran. And once I'd left, I didn't know how to come back."

"You were my best friend, Risa," Cat said quietly. "You could have told me. Whatever it was, I would have understood."

"Not this." Cat had always been the good girl, silently disapproving of some of Risa's wilder escapades and her seemingly casual attitude toward sex. But she'd always stayed a loyal friend. Risa doubted Cat would have been as understanding if she knew the whole truth of why Risa had left Luna Hermosa.

"Risa..." Her expression softening, Cat reached over

and took Risa's hand. "You're a good person. You've just never believed it."

With tears threatening and her throat suddenly thick, Risa leaned over to hug her. Cat hugged her back, and they stayed that way for a few moments. "I'm sorry...for everything," Risa said. She hastily wiped at her eyes. "I hope we can start over. I'd like us to be friends again."

"I'd like that, too. I really missed you."

"I missed you, too. I hate that we've lost so much time."

Cat waved off her further apologies. "We'll just have to make up for it. You can start by telling me what you've been doing since you got back. You know, with the shelter, your family...Ry Kincaid."

"Why do I get the feeling you aren't as interested in the first two subjects as you are in the last?"

"Probably because I've heard more gossip about him and you than I have anything else," Cat said with a laugh. "So tell me—how much of it is true?"

"It depends on what you've heard," Risa hedged.

"That you've been lovers almost from the first minute he got into town. Del Garrett's been telling everyone she caught you and him at the shelter one day, doing, as she put it, unmentionable things in broad daylight in front of God, her aunt Clara and anyone else who happened to be walking by."

Risa felt her face get hot. "That's not exactly true."

"Which part?"

"You know how Del embellishes things," Risa muttered.

"So you are lovers."

"It's more than that." Much more, at least on her side, and maybe it was wishful thinking, but she thought it might be more for Ry, too. Things had been better between them since the sledding outing, and she had started to hope that maybe they'd continue that way.

"I can see it is for you," Cat said. She touched Risa's hand again. "Be careful, okay? People are saying he's a lot like his father, and a guy like that could really hurt you."

"Ry wouldn't hurt me. And don't believe everything you hear. He's nothing like Jed." She repeated the same defense she'd been using over and over with Aria, Cruz, Cort, her father and practically everyone else.

She started to shift the subject to the changes in Cat's life over the years, but a heavy tread on the staircase interrupted. Giving Cat's hand a quick squeeze, she murmured, "Be right back," and went to see who it was, only to find herself caught in Ry's arms the second she stepped outside her office.

He muffled her surprised exclamation with his mouth on hers, taking advantage of her parted lips to kiss her deeply. Lost in the pleasure of being with him again, Risa forgot about where she was and Cat waiting behind her until a small cough pulled her back to reality.

"I need to get going," Cat said, smiling when they turned to her. "It's nice to see you again," she added to Ry, who nodded. Then turning back to Risa, she said, "Let's get together again soon and really catch up."

"It's a date, I promise," Risa told her. They hugged again, Cat leaving them with a little wave and a wink for Risa.

"Looks like you two made up," Ry commented as he pulled her close again.

Risa tugged down the zipper of his jacket, wanting to be nearer to his warmth. He looked so good to her after the days apart and felt even better. "We're good again, I think. How'd your jobs go?"

"Not bad. Great weather, good pay. The skiing was fine. One problem, though."

"What's that?"

"I woke up every morning with Bear instead of you." Cupping her face in one hand, he searched her eyes a moment, rubbing his thumb over her lips, then bent and kissed her, this time slowly and with a tenderness that strengthened her wish she could be more to him than a lover and a friend.

"You got plans for the weekend?" he asked, shifting his kisses along a path from her cheek to the sensitive spot below her ear.

"Not yet. I was waiting for you. Did you have anything particular in mind?" She smiled to herself, knowing exactly what he was thinking.

"Thought I might grab some supplies and spend a few days at the cabin. Clean up…" He settled his hands on her hips, drawing her against him. "Find something to unpack. You know, the usual."

She sighed, pretending disappointment. "Well, if that's what you want. I hope you and Bear enjoy yourselves."

Her attempt to twist out of his hold ended quickly. Ry scooped her up, carried her into the office, kicked the door shut behind them and sat her on the couch. Taking seconds to strip off his jacket, he joined her there, catching her in an embrace that left no doubt he didn't intend to spend the weekend cleaning and unpacking.

"I'm not planning on waking up tomorrow with Bear," he rumbled after finally letting her up for air.

Her smile reflecting her bubbling happiness, Risa pulled him to her for another kiss. "Me, either," she said.

* * *

He didn't want to leave her, but half an hour later, Ry found himself alone and with hours on his hands before he could pick up Risa and head back to the cabin. He'd tried to persuade her into taking an extended lunch. But, her day completely full and already behind after his and Cat's visits, she'd reluctantly turned him down. He'd had to be satisfied with her promise to thoroughly welcome him home this evening.

Split between imagining the ways he wanted to show her how much he'd missed her, and halfheartedly making a mental list of the things he needed to get done before tonight, he nearly missed the muffled bark of his cell phone. He fished it out of his inside jacket pocket, resigned to answering when he recognized Duran's number.

"I heard you were back," Duran said. "I was wondering if you had time to grab lunch. I wanted to talk to you about a couple of things."

"Am I under surveillance?" Ry grumbled. "I just got in about an hour ago."

Duran laughed. "Cat Esteban is a pediatric nurse at the hospital. She told Lia she ran into you at the shelter, and Lia called me. So what about lunch?"

Ry almost said no. But being with Risa had changed him in more ways than one, and if he was going to stay in Luna Hermosa, for the business and for her, he couldn't keep pretending that didn't include having some sort of relationship with his brothers. "Where and when?"

"How about noon at Morente's?" Duran said, naming the upscale restaurant in town owned by Sawyer and Cort's grandparents. "I've taken a short break from filming, but I've got some errands to run before then."

"Yeah, sure," Ry agreed. Morente's wasn't his

choice, but he figured he could tolerate it for the hour or so they'd be there. At least he wouldn't have to worry about Bear; he'd left his dog with Risa, knowing Bear would be more content staying with her than cooped up in the Jeep the better part of the day.

He used the time until noon to run a few errands of his own and got to Morente's the same time Duran was pulling into the parking lot.

"You know, getting you here was almost too easy," Duran teased as they started inside.

Ry shrugged. "Risa tells me I need to work on my people skills. I'm practicing."

An attractive dark-haired woman, in figure-hugging black that showed her curves to advantage and left no doubt she was soon expecting a baby, met them at the front, greeting Duran with a hug. "I heard you'd run off and left your woman alone for the week. Aren't you supposed to be getting ready for a wedding?"

"Noah and I needed the rest of our clothes. Believe me, the sooner I can finish the move from L.A., the better. I don't know if you've met my brother," he said, indicating Ry standing a few paces behind him. "Ry, this is Nova Tréjos. She and Lia are old friends."

"Watch the 'old' part, honey," Nova told him with a wink. She gave Ry an appreciative once-over. "I've heard all about you."

"Who hasn't?" Ry muttered.

Nova tossed him a grin over her shoulder as she led them to a corner table. "Oh, I'm sure there are one or two people left in town who haven't. But don't worry, in a month or two, we'll have something new to gossip about and you'll be old news."

"I didn't know you were gone this week, too," Ry

said to Duran after Nova had left them and the waitress took their order.

"I'm trying to get everything wrapped up in L.A. before the wedding. I finished packing up my apartment there this week, and I had everything but the furniture moved to the ranch. It's going to have to wait until Lia and I settle on a house. We found a few places we like, but we haven't made a final decision yet." Duran paused to take a drink of his beer. "That's part of what I wanted to talk to you about—the wedding. It's not going to be anything too formal, just a lot of family and friends. I'd like you to be there. You and Risa," he added.

"I gotta give you credit," he said, leaning back in his chair. "At least you didn't warn me away from her. Unlike most everyone else."

"That's mostly Aria's doing. Although in her defense, she's just worried about her sister."

"So Cruz says. Maybe she should back off and let Risa decide for herself what she wants or doesn't want."

"From what little I know, Risa's had some trouble in the past, and Aria is concerned she'll end up hurt again."

"What happened with Risa was a long time ago, and it doesn't make a damned bit of difference now." Ry heard himself, sharper than he'd intended, and he knew he was letting his own issues with Risa's past color his reaction. He forced a more level tone. "If Risa trusts me not to hurt her, that should be good enough for everyone else."

"Does she?"

"What?"

"Trust that you're not going to hurt her."

"Yeah, she does. But she's the only one." From the start, she'd been the one who'd trusted, befriended, defended him. She'd taught him about caring and had shaken his belief that he'd never have all the things he was denied growing up: home, a family, love. He needed to remind himself of that when he was tempted to dwell on her confessions to him, the secrets she'd trusted him with, him and no one else.

"It sounds like you two have gotten pretty close," Duran said.

Ry lifted a shoulder in response, avoiding his brother's speculative gaze, fidgeting with his beer glass.

"Okay, not my business. And if Risa trusts you, that is good enough for me." Ry looked up, and Duran smiled a little. "Despite what you may think, I am on your side. So, about the wedding—"

"I'll be there," Ry said abruptly.

Duran reached in his shirt pocket and pulled out a cream-colored envelope, handing it over to Ry. "Your official invitation. I meant what I said, too. Bring Risa. And Ry—I'm glad you're coming."

Surprising himself Ry said, "Me, too." And even more surprising, found that he meant it.

Ry got to the shelter a little after five and immediately saw something was wrong.

Risa was standing next to a parked car, talking to an older couple and a girl who appeared to Ry to be in her late teens. Their tense stances, Risa's intent expression as she spoke to the trio, and the look of the girl—arms wrapped tightly around her body, a defeated droop to her posture—told him he didn't need to be in the middle of this.

He waited until the couple and the girl had left before

getting out of the Jeep and walking up to where Risa stood. "Everything okay?"

"I hope so," she said, almost to herself, her eyes still fixed on the recently vacated driveway. With a little shake, she sighed and looked up at him. "Give me a few minutes, and I'll be ready to go."

It was much later, after they'd gotten back to the cabin, that she told him what had happened.

"Thanks for putting up with my mood," she said. They had just finished dinner and were settled in front of the fireplace. Her head resting on his shoulder, she drew idle patterns on his chest, an alternative nervous gesture to twisting at her ring. She'd recently taken it up whenever they were together and something was bothering her. "I get these cases sometimes, these girls who remind me of myself….I shouldn't let it get to me, but it does."

"And this girl…" he prompted.

"She's eighteen. She got pregnant at a party after sleeping with a guy she barely knows. She turned up this afternoon and wanted a place to stay because she was afraid to tell her parents."

"Guess you convinced her to call them."

She nodded. "I know how she feels, but it's worse trying to do it alone, whether she keeps the baby or not. Her parents were actually pretty good about it. I think they'll be supportive no matter what she does. She might even decide later to tell the father, although she was pretty dead set against it today."

Ry didn't comment, but in the darkest hours of the night, holding her while she slept, peacefulness eluded him. Gently, so as not to disturb her, he eased out of bed. Finding his jeans in the piled clothing on the floor, he pulled them on and went into the living room. He stirred up the fire and then sat on the couch, watching the flickering light and shadows. Bear, roused by the slight sounds, lumbered over to plop down next to him, and Ry roughed the fur behind the dog's ears, seeking comfort in the familiar gesture.

"Hey…" The soft query pulled him out of his thoughts. Risa, wrapped in a blanket, hovered at the edge of the room. "What's wrong?"

He gestured her over, noticing she sat down next to him instead of curling up against him as usual. "Couldn't sleep. Guess I'm not used to a real bed yet."

"No…" She studied him a moment, then said, "It's me, isn't it? It's been me for a while now. What I said about giving up my baby and never telling the father bothers you. And that girl today was just another reminder."

"I'm not—" he started, then stopped, uncomfortable with having to voice feelings he'd rather not have had in the first place and not sure how to explain them to her. "Okay, yeah, it does. Knowing that…coming here and having to deal with the family thing and settle with things in the past I'd rather forget—I'm trying to understand. But it's not easy."

"I shouldn't have told you. I just…I wanted to tell someone. I thought, we were—close, and that if anybody could accept me, it would be you."

"Risa…" He touched her face, looked into her eyes and hated the layer of vulnerability and guilt he'd added there. "I'm not sorry you told me. It's not you. It's me."

"It's me, too. You think I should have told the father."

"He had a right to know. Maybe it would have made a difference."

"You think it would have made a difference if Jed had

known about you and Duran?" she challenged. "Jed knew Cruz's mother was pregnant, and it didn't stop him from abandoning her and ignoring you for thirty-five years. I doubt he would have been any different if he'd known about you and Duran. The father of my baby would have been the same way. He wasn't much older than me, and he would have been all too ready to avoid any responsibility for me or a baby. Even now I'm not convinced he'd want to know."

"You don't know that for sure," he countered, defensive because he knew she was right, at least about Jed, and that doubled his own abandonment. To avoid thinking about it, he flung out the other question that had been weighing heavily on his mind. "Weren't you curious, after you gave him up? Did you ever try to find out what happened to him?"

Risa clutched the blanket more tightly around herself. She didn't move, but Ry could almost feel her withdraw from him. "I thought he would be better off with a couple who wanted a child than with me."

"You don't know if he was adopted by the right people. What if he ended up like me?"

"This isn't about you, Ry," she shot back. Her eyes filled with tears, and she angrily swiped them aside. "I did what I thought was the right thing at the time. Maybe it wasn't, but it was the best I could do. Believe me, I've been paying for it ever since. You can't make me feel any guiltier than I already do."

Confronted with the realization he'd hurt her, that he'd done the one thing he'd told her and everyone else he wouldn't do, Ry's need for answers faded. He tried to reach out to her.

She avoided his hand and jerked to her feet. "This is

the reason I've never told anyone else what happened. I knew no one would ever accept it. They'd be just like you and want to know how I could do what I did. They'd want to know who the father was, and they'd be looking at everyone in town I'd ever been with and wondering, and talking. And if they found out who he was, it would be impossible with us both living here. Either way, it would mess up several people's lives, and that would be my fault, too."

Ry stood up, feeling it like a punch to his gut when she took a step away from him. "I'm sorry. That's not...I never meant you to feel that way."

"I'm sorry, too," she said, her voice shaking and the tears trailing down her cheeks. "I'm sorry I ever told you, and I'm sorry about every rotten thing that ever happened to you. But I can't go back and fix it all. I thought—I'd hoped—you understood and could accept it. It's obvious you don't or can't."

"I want to," he said. "I don't want this between us."

"I don't, either. But I don't know how to make it go away." The fight drained out of her, leaving her looking pale and tired. "Maybe it's better if I leave."

"No." His denial came out so forcefully her eyes widened in surprise. Through with the distance between them, he eliminated it in one stride and circled one arm around her, gently brushing away her tears with his free hand. "I'm lousy at this relationship thing. But I don't want to lose you," he said gruffly. "It's never mattered before because I never cared. Now it's...I need you. So if I screw up, just—don't leave."

It was probably the most inarticulate confession of feelings anyone had ever made, but Risa seemed to understand. She laid her palm against his face, and the way she looked at him, the emotion in her eyes both intense and tender and so unlike anything he'd ever known, put another crack in his defensive walls.

"I won't leave," she vowed softly.

Ry gathered her against him, holding her tightly, and it was a long time before either of them were willing to let go.

Chapter Fourteen

"*Shoosh* and glide, that's all there is to it," Ry coaxed. He had taught dozens of people to cross-country ski, but Dolores was the most skittish, sure she'd never master the skill. Glancing back to where Risa was working with Gustavo, teaching him how to navigate the snowy path, Risa's smile encouraged him to keep trying. "Think of it this way. Learning to ski is like learning to use a new tool. It's intimidating at first, but once you learn to use it, it opens up all kinds of different doors."

Risa skied up beside them. "Ry's right. If you conquer this fear, you can use that tool to conquer others."

"I don't think I can," Dolores said. "What if I fall?"

Ry began to lean, waver, flap his hands in an exaggerated motion, teetering on the edges of his skis. Gustavo and the other children started to laugh and point fingers at him, egging him on to make an even bigger show of tumbling over in a pillow of white fluff. The kids and Sarah and Wendy laughed even harder when he hit the ground. Ry brushed the snow from his face and jacket and pulled himself back up. "That's what happens if you fall. You fall and you get back up."

"C'mon, Mom, look at me," Gustavo bragged, gliding ahead of the group.

Her son's fearlessness didn't inspire Dolores. She stayed stiffly in place, refusing to move.

"Why don't you all go on ahead, circle the trail through the park," Risa told the others. "We'll catch up with you."

They'd started out early on the crisp, sunny Saturday morning, heading out to the city park to take a lesson in cross-country skiing. Originally, Ry suggested an ice hike in the mountains, but Risa had talked him out of it, convincing him it was too soon for her group to tackle that kind of challenge.

Once he and Risa agreed on the cross-country confidence-building effort, Ry called friends and managed to pick up several sets of used cross-country skis, poles and boots from ski swaps in Santa Fe, Taos and Angel Fire.

Most of the kids were beside themselves with excitement this morning, and the moms—even Wendy, the most timid of them—were willing to go along. Dolores, the one Ry figured would lead the group, had surprisingly been the one to balk.

"Okay, here's what we're gonna do." He gestured to Risa, and the two of them moved to either side of Dolores. "We'll be your support until you get the hang of it."

"You can do this," Risa said. "I know you can."

Ry planted a pole in the snow and moved his left ski a few inches ahead. "Six inches. Just move one ski six inches forward."

Dolores looked at him, then at Risa. Following Risa's example, he answered with a reassuring smile. Tightly clenching her poles, Dolores edged one ski up.

"Perfect. Move it back…now the other one." When Dolores tentatively obeyed, Ry nodded. "Slide your foot forward like you're taking a step."

Hesitating, Dolores stared hard at her feet. After a long pause, she gritted her teeth and pushed one ski over the soft powder.

"Plant your pole ahead in the snow and do the same with your other ski," Risa said, demonstrating as she spoke.

Accomplishing the task, Dolores's face cleared. "Am I skiing?"

"You got it," Ry said. "That's all there is to it."

"*Shoosh* and glide," Dolores muttered to herself, making her skis do what her mouth ordered. "*Shoosh* and glide." She moved out a few feet ahead of Ry and Risa. Then, realizing she'd lost her two supports and panicking, she looked back.

"You're fine." Ry waved her on. "And what happens if you fall?"

Dolores smiled. "I brush the snow off and get up."

"Exactly." Ry moved beside her, showing her as he told her what to do next. "Nice and easy. Slide a little, then walk a bit, and slide again when you're ready."

"We're right behind you," Risa assured the other woman. "Just go at your own pace."

They watched Dolores make her way up the trail, gaining more confidence with each stride.

"I think you should be doing my job," Risa said, shaking her head and smiling at Dolores's progress.

"Not hardly. I've been playing in the snow and giving

a few lessons. You're the one who sets the example for them, makes them believe in themselves."

Risa's smile faded. She looked in the direction of the giant old cottonwood in the center of the park, now barren of leaves and laden with snow. "I'm no role model."

"What's that supposed to mean?"

"It means I'm hardly a good example of decision making and taking responsibility. I spend a lot of time telling my clients they need to overcome their fears and their pasts, but all I've done is run from mine."

"You aren't running now. You came back here even though you knew what you'd be up against." Ry cupped her face in his hand, rubbing his thumb against her cheek. "That doesn't seem cowardly to me."

She didn't answer. After a moment, they started after Dolores, skiing in silence for a bit, fresh winter air nipping at their cheeks and noses, body heat from their exertion filling their jackets and gloves. The exercise felt therapeutic, a tension reliever, yet Ry couldn't relax.

He was the reason behind her renewed self-doubts. He'd upset her with his reaction to her confession, and though he'd deliberately shoved aside his issues and questions, both of them knew he hadn't resolved them. Because of that, he sensed there was something she hadn't told him and that she was struggling over whether or not she should, probably afraid of his response.

"Whatever it is," he said abruptly, voicing what he wanted to believe, "it can't be anywhere near as bad as you think."

"Ry…" Her expression troubled, she stopped, tried again. "There's something—"

"Hey, slowpokes," Dolores called to them. "We're all going to beat you to the end if you don't hurry!"

"That's what you think," Ry shot back.

Risa started to increase her pace. "We should get moving."

"Wait." Ry maneuvered in front of her, blocking the path. "I want to clear this up, once and for all, while we're still out of hearing range of the others."

"I want that, too," she said softly. "I just don't know if…"

"If I'm gonna react like a jerk?"

"It's not that."

"Risa, look, if you want to tell me, I'll listen. If you don't, then I don't need to hear it. Either way, we'll work through it."

"Is that what you really want?" He looked at her, questioning, and she added, "To work through it?"

Leaning over his skis, he moved close enough to kiss her, slowly and thoroughly. "Yeah, that's what I want."

She nodded, yet uncertainty remained in her eyes. He would have liked to get her alone, convince her it was true, but the others were waiting and there wasn't time or space.

When they caught up with Dolores, he challenged her. "Wanna race?"

Wide-eyed, Dolores shook her head vehemently. "No, no, not me. This is fast enough for me. I was only joking."

"I guess it's you and me, then," Ry said to Risa.

"Oh, yeah?"

"Yeah. Unless you're afraid of losing…" As he'd guessed, he'd struck her competitive nerve. With a flash of a smile, she darted out ahead of him.

Giving her a safe lead, he followed, cheers and whoops accompanying them as they sped by.

He pumped the skis, jammed the poles and rocketed

ahead, cold wind frosting his face, making him feel alive, strong. Strong enough to undo the hurt.

Risa finished helping Dolores tuck her exhausted and happy little boy into bed. Outside the bedroom, she reached out to hug Dolores. "You and Gustavo and the others did so well today. Ry and I are so proud of all of you. And you should be proud of you, too."

"*Gracias,* but it's because of you. You and Ry, you're changing our lives."

"You're doing that on your own," Risa said. "Look at you—when you first came here, you thought getting away from Rael would be impossible. But you did it, you and Gustavo."

"We did, didn't we?"

"And today you did something else that seemed next to impossible."

Dolores lifted her chin and smiled. "I skied!"

"You let go of your fear," Risa said, smiling back. "Like Ry said, you got a new tool today. One you can use every day."

"You two are so good together," Dolores said. She shook a gentle finger at Risa. "I heard a little of your talking today when you were skiing behind me. *Lo siento,* sorry, I didn't mean to. Whatever is going on between you, don't lose him. Talk, pray. Whatever it takes, because believe me, he is one in a million, *el mejor,* the best."

Although probably not very professional, Risa had never been able to stick to a strictly impersonal relationship with her clients, and at the moment, she was feeling vulnerable, a feeling she knew Dolores well understood. "Yes, he is," she agreed. "And I don't want to lose him.

But if something happens to Ry and me, I'll still be here. The shelter won't change. You and Gustavo and the others will have a safe place here for as long as you need."

"That, I already knew," Dolores said, giving Risa's hand a squeeze.

They said their good-nights, and Risa walked back to the front of the house, considering Dolores's words as she got ready to leave and meet Ry at his cabin. Ry was the best thing that had ever happened to her. And he deserved the best from her.

He deserved the truth, all of it.

She tried to shake the foreboding that it could destroy them. She told herself they were strong enough to overcome it.

And all the way to the cabin, she did exactly what Delores had recommended.

She prayed.

He didn't answer her tap at the door, and Risa let herself inside. Bear greeted her, bumping her leg until she bent and scratched him behind the ears. Leaving her coat and purse behind, she found Ry stretched out on the couch next to a blazing fire.

Bare-chested, wearing only his flannel sweats, he appeared to be sleeping until she bent over him and lightly kissed his mouth. "Looks like somebody fell asleep without me."

"No, just resting," he said, shrugging off her raised brow. "Thought you might be tired, too. First runs of the season are always kickers. You're going to hear a lot of moaning around the shelter tomorrow."

"I'll be the first. My thighs are burning already."

Ry reached a lazy hand to brush her leg. "They

look hot, that's for sure. Especially in those tight little ski pants."

Risa longed to respond to his touch, lose herself in their lovemaking and forget her resolution to be completely honest with him. If she did, though, she would never tell him. She had to do this before cowardice set in again.

"I need to talk to you about something," she said.

"First things first," he murmured, sliding both his hands up her legs.

Gently, she disengaged from his hold and sat down beside him. "This needs to be first."

"If this is about earlier," he said, shifting upright, "forget it. It's not worth you getting upset again."

"I can't. You deserve to know."

"Whatever it is, I don't care." He gently brushed the hair from her cheek, the tenderness of his touch nearly undoing her. "What I care about is you. Only you."

"I care about you, too. I know you've had doubts about me, because I haven't been completely honest with you."

"Maybe I have, but that's my problem, not yours."

"It's mine, too, because if you can't completely trust me, if you're always wondering what it is I haven't said, what I've done, then we aren't going to be able to work things through."

His silence confirmed it for her. Drawing in a deep breath, she said, "When we first met, I never expected we'd end up together. You were here to come to terms with your family, and I didn't want to get in the way of that. Unfortunately, I did, right from the start."

"That worked both ways, you know," he said softly.

"I guess."

"No guessing about it. But your family or mine, I don't give a damn what any of them think. We're what matters."

Oh, she wanted to believe that. She needed to believe it. "I hope you still think that's true when I tell you."

Ry took her hand, linking them together. "Tell me what?"

"Who fathered my baby," she said, barely able to voice more than a whisper.

"Risa, I don't…" His fingers flexed against hers, and the motion telegraphed the apprehension she saw in his face. "Maybe this isn't the best idea."

"No, I need to say it." Quickly, as if by hastening it out she could lessen the inevitable blow, she said, "It was Josh. Josh was my baby's father."

Chapter Fifteen

Ry stared at her, blindsided by her revelation. "Josh...
My brother Josh?"

"Yes." She got to her feet and began pacing the
confines of the living room, agitating her ring in quick,
jerky motions. "We dated for a few months, although
usually our idea of a date was sex and a couple of beers."
Her short harsh laugh made him wince. "It's funny. I
was Josh's first. No one would ever believe that, because
later, before Eliana, he was the one that went through
women like he was trying to set a new record."

He didn't say anything, not sure how to respond, and
Risa, after a glance in his direction, shook her head.

"We weren't especially careful. Back then, we were
both reckless. We didn't think about the consequences.
And, well...you know the rest." After a pause, she
added, "I didn't want to tell you it was Josh because I

didn't want to make things between you and your family more difficult than they already are."

"Yeah, it's…" Difficult didn't begin to describe it. Ry stood, unable to stay seated, and ended up in front of the fireplace. He fisted his hands against the mantle, struggling with a turmoil of emotion. That Risa's child—another unwanted baby—was his nephew somehow made things worse. Though there weren't strong bonds between him and his brothers, he couldn't shake his uneasiness at knowing there was a kid out there—a blood relation—that might have ended up like him.

"I'll tell Josh." Risa quietly dropped the words into the strained silence.

He turned to where she stood opposite him. The resignation, almost defeat, in her face added another combatant to his inner conflict.

"I've been running long enough," she said. "It's never going to be over. I won't find any resolution with my family until I tell everyone the truth."

"When you tell him, I'll go with you."

"No. I can do this myself. I should have done it a long time ago. Maybe then…" With a sharp shake, she let her gaze drop.

Ry strode over to her and clasped her shoulders. "I'm going with you. Like you said, you shouldn't have to do it alone."

He thought she would refuse him again. Instead, she half shrugged, and he chose to take that as acceptance. His hands moved to hold her, but she pulled away.

Going to where she'd left her jacket, she put it on and fumbled in her purse for her keys. "I'll call you as soon as I set up a time to meet with Josh."

"You don't need to leave. It's late—"

"I can't stay." She rubbed her fingers over her temple, and he saw the tremor in her hand, the stiff way she held herself as if struggling to keep herself together.

"Then I'm following you home."

"No, Ry, don't. Just don't." Spinning around, she yanked open the door and was outside before he could stop her.

Her abrupt departure left him rooted in place until he heard her car start. The sound spurred him to action. Moving quickly, he threw on jeans, boots and a sweatshirt, checked that Bear was settled for the night with food and water, and searched out his own keys and coat. By the time he got to the Jeep and was on the road back to town, she had a fifteen-minute head start. It didn't bother him, at first, until he reached the city limits and there was no sign of her.

He took her usual route home, but her car wasn't in the driveway. Uneasiness gripped him hard. Not giving himself time to consider his options, he parked the Jeep and strode up to the house.

The older man who answered his knock looked slightly perplexed at what he must have thought at first was a stranger on his doorstep. "Can I help you?"

"Hello Mr. Charez. I'm looking for Risa."

"Ah…" He looked more closely at Ry. "Oh, I remember you now, you're Jed's son. Risa's not here. I thought she was with you."

"She was," Ry said grimly. "She decided to go home. I wanted to be sure she got here. But I can't find her."

Joseph studied him a moment, then stepped back. "You'd better come in."

Accepting the offer, Ry followed the other man into the large living room. Joseph gestured him to a chair, and though he wasn't in the mood to waste time chatting, Ry needed the older man's help, so he shed his coat and sat down.

"Risa won't talk to me much about you," Joseph said. "But it's obvious she cares a lot about you. What happened tonight?"

"We talked about something that upset her. She didn't want to stay."

"I'm guessing you aren't going to tell me what you talked about."

"No, that's up to her." He wasn't about to betray Risa's confidence to her father.

"She told you, didn't she, about why she left, what's been hurting her all these years." It wasn't a question. When Ry stayed silent, Joseph, sighing, ran a hand over his buzz of graying hair, his face weary. "When she was a girl, Risa would disappear, for hours sometimes, when something upset her. She hated for anyone to see her cry. I think she wanted everyone to think she was tough, that nothing bothered her. But I see now that she was the most vulnerable of any of us." His steady gaze met Ry's. "You won't find her until she's ready to come back."

"Where would she go?" Ry pressed, not willing to accept that Risa was alone somewhere, hurting and bereft of comfort.

"I don't know, but it won't be anywhere either of us could think to look for her."

"Isn't there someone in town she'd—"

"No," Joseph said with a finality that was weighted with sorrow. "There's no one. I thought maybe she'd found someone in you. She seemed happier lately." He shook his head, then made to stand up. "You can stay here, if you like. She'll probably be back by morning."

Probably wasn't good enough. Ry didn't want to imagine what he would feel like if she didn't come back. He hated sitting around and doing nothing, but he didn't know what else to do apart from taking off and scouring the area in the hope he'd stumble across her.

"Thanks," he said at last to Joseph, who was waiting for his answer. "I'll stay."

He refused Joseph's offer of a bed for the night, and instead, after Joseph retired to his own bedroom, camped in the chair and listened for the slightest sound that would tell him Risa was safely home.

It was after seven, after a long, sleepless night, that he was finally rewarded for his vigilance. The rest of the household was already up, so he went outside to meet her. She looked like hell, pale and drawn, her hair tangled and her jeans patched with grime, as if she'd been kneeling in the dirt. The urge to grab her up, shelter her in his arms and never let her go was nearly irresistible. But he held his ground, sure she'd bolt if he tried.

Seeing him, she stopped midway to the door. "What are you doing here?"

"Waiting for you. It was that or come looking for you, and your dad told me that wouldn't have done me any good. When you didn't come home—"

She put up her hand to ward off any reply he might have made. "I talked to Josh. I'm meeting him at his place in a couple of hours."

"Then I'll go to the cabin and grab a shower and be back to pick you up. Don't bother arguing," he said when her mouth opened in what he knew would be a protest.

She nodded instead, and that left them facing each other with a thousand things unspoken between them.

Her distance from him was more than physical, but he

could only make the strides to close the gap of space. She stiffened, though she didn't move away, only looked at him with eyes that were red-rimmed and dark with pain.

Very gently, Ry brushed the hair from her face, bending to kiss her forehead. A shudder went through her, and for brief seconds, she leaned into his touch.

Then she suddenly turned from him and quickly walked into the house, leaving him there, watching her until she was gone.

She wasn't ready for this, but she never would be.

Josh had greeted her and Ry easily enough, ushering them into the living room, but she could tell he was confused as to the reason she'd wanted this meeting, and why she'd brought Ry with her. Resigned to Ry's insistence on being here with her, she doubted his presence would make telling Josh any easier.

Risa half wished Eliana hadn't been there, either, except she supposed it didn't matter. After today, everyone would know the truth. Besides, as Josh's wife, she had a right to be there.

"I gotta admit, you kinda caught me off guard when you called, Risa," Josh said, sitting next to his wife while Risa took the chair across from them, Ry standing next to her. "I'm guessin' this isn't a visit to talk over old times."

"In a way it is. Only not in the way you mean." The nervousness, dread even, she expected never materialized. Instead, she felt empty, drained of any emotion except a dull resignation. Maybe she had purged it last night, when she had driven miles and miles, stopping only after the tears blurred her vision so much she couldn't see the road and she was physically sick from the upheaval. "I never told you the reason why, all those years ago, I broke things off with you and ran away."

Josh exchanged a glance with Eliana. "I figured you were havin' trouble at home."

"I was pregnant," she said flatly. "With your baby."

"My—" Eliana stared at him, eyes wide, but Josh's attention was riveted on Risa. His expression hardened. "How do you know it was mine? It's not like you were real selective back then about who you were with."

Before Risa could retort, Ry intervened. "Back off," he warned in a low, tight voice. "She doesn't get anything from telling you the truth."

Josh glared at his brother, unmoved by Ry's threatening stance, until Eliana grasped her husband's arm. He glanced at her and briefly touched her hand. Then his eyes whipped back to Risa.

"If it is true, why didn't you tell me?" he demanded.

"Why? You wouldn't have wanted him then. In fact, you once told me back then you'd never be able to settle down, have kids, get married. And you can't tell me your parents wouldn't have done everything they could to hush the whole thing up, especially your dad."

Not countering her directly, Josh asked instead, "What happened to him?"

"She doesn't know," Ry said.

Stung, Risa refused to look at him. She couldn't—not and keep her emotions in check. "I gave him up for adoption."

"Without tellin' me," Josh said with a grimace. He jerked to his feet, shoving a hand through his hair. Pacing a few steps, he spun toward Risa. "I'm gonna find him."

"Josh—" Eliana started. She stopped, her expression troubled as she looked between her husband and Risa.

"I don't think that's a good idea," Risa said.

"The hell it isn't. I wanna know what happened to my son."

"He's got a right to know." Ry backed his brother. "I'd think you'd want to do the same."

The accusation struck like a blow, and Risa flinched. "You both need to think about the boy," she said, forcing her voice to stay steady. "He's twelve now. Do you really want to disrupt his life?"

"Depends on what kind of life he's got," Ry said. "Just because someone adopted him doesn't mean he ended up in a good place."

"I'm damn well gonna find out," Josh snapped. He turned to Risa. "Are you gonna help me?"

Both he and Ry looked at her, and under the weight of their combined indictment, something broke between her and Ry: his promise not to hurt her shattered into a million irretrievable pieces.

She couldn't think about that now because the pain would cripple her, and she needed what courage she had left. Sucking in a shaky breath, she made herself look back at the two men. "I'll do what I can. I know where to start, at least." She stood up, feeling as if the last minutes had aged her, leaving her stiff and cold. "I'll make some calls on Monday and let you know what I find out."

She didn't wait for Josh's reply or to see if Ry would follow her but walked swiftly out of the room, snatching up her coat, not bothering to put it on until she was through the door and down the front steps.

"Risa!"

Ry called her from behind, but she kept walking. She couldn't hear any more of what he had to say right now. He'd made his choice, and it wasn't her.

"Risa, stop." He grasped her arm to break her stride. "I'll take you home."

"No, thanks. I'll get a ride."

"Don't be so stubborn," he said, scowling. "I brought you, I'll take you back."

"I'm not going back with you. You told me I didn't have to do this alone, Ry. Well, you were wrong. I do. Starting with this."

They stood face-to-face in a silent battle of wills, and unpredictably it was him that surrendered. Rubbing a hand over his face, he blew out a breath. "I shouldn't have said what I did back there. I'm sorry."

"No, you're not," Risa said. "You meant what you said—you always do." She bit her lip hard and had to look away. "That's one of the things I love about you, your honesty and how you don't pretend to be something you're not."

"I don't know how to fix this," he said, his voice rough at the edges.

"Maybe you can't."

She couldn't decipher his expression. Regret mixed with anger, layered with resolve and something akin to desperation. "I can't leave it like this. Let me take you home."

It was easier to give in than to stand in the gray cold and argue. But as she nodded and began walking back to the Jeep with him, she thought that no matter how much he wanted to, or what he tried, there were some broken things that he couldn't repair.

Chapter Sixteen

In telling Ry and Josh about her baby, the worst was over.

The drive from Josh's ranch to her father's house had been bad enough. Neither of them had said anything. Ry was focused on the road, gripping the steering wheel so hard she thought it might crack. She huddled in her corner, keeping as much distance as possible between them. She escaped the second the Jeep quit moving, closing the passenger door on anything he might have said, and he made no attempt to follow her.

Barely inside the house, she had her cell phone out, calling Aria.

"Thanks for taking time off work," she told her sister when, half an hour later, Aria arrived. "I wouldn't have bothered you if it weren't important."

"It's okay. I'm worried, though. What's going on? Is it the shelter?"

Risa shook her head and turned from her sister to her dad. "No, that's running fairly smoothly." She shifted in the familiar worn easy chair where she sat facing the other two in her father's living room. "This is personal."

Joseph leaned forward. "What is it, honey? You're not ill, are you?"

"No, Dad, it's…it's about a long time ago, what I should have told you then." Her breath shook. Facing her father and her sister, admitting what she'd done, owning up to her shame, was probably the hardest thing she'd ever attempted, save for telling Ry and Josh. But she had made the decision to do this. If she didn't, she'd never be able to move forward. And she certainly didn't want her family learning about it from any of Josh's family, once Josh told them. "It has to do with Josh and me."

"Josh Garrett?" Joseph frowned. "I didn't think you and he had seen much of each other since high school."

"Oh, Risa, don't say you and Josh…" Aria covered her eyes with a hand.

"Don't be ridiculous," Risa snapped, more harshly than she had a right to. After all, in the past, stealing someone else's lover might not have been out of her range of sins. When total confusion contorted the faces of Aria and her father, she decided the only way to say it was bluntly.

"I slept around a lot in high school, more than you probably know," she said. Her father winced, and Aria's mouth tightened. "I ran away because I ended up pregnant. With Josh's baby."

Anger, disappointment, disbelief, compassion, all struggled for mastery of Aria's expression. "It can't be. Not Josh."

"*Madre de Dios*, Risa…" Joseph gestured helplessly

at his youngest daughter. "Why didn't you tell us? We could have helped you. Instead—I don't want to think about where you ended up."

"Eventually, in a shelter in Albuquerque," Risa said. The renewed memories flooded back, and she kept them to herself, unwilling to burden her father with them. "That's why, when they asked me to open a shelter here, I agreed. They took me in when I didn't have anyone else."

"You had your family. How could you think we would have abandoned you?"

"Oh, Dad, I never thought that. I know you loved me. I just…I never thought I deserved it," Risa finished miserably. She stared down at her hands. "I always felt I could never measure up to any of you. I had something to prove, and it was that everyone was right, I would never be good enough." The sound she made in her throat was half sob, half mirthless laughter. "I did a pretty good job of it, too."

"I should have known. I should have listened to you more, paid more attention," Joseph said, almost to himself. "You were so headstrong, so defiant. Your mother and I, we thought it was your way of growing up. We never dreamed—"

"It's not your fault, Dad. They were my mistakes. I was old enough to understand the consequences."

"You weren't old enough to deal with them all by yourself," Aria said quietly. "And Dad's right. We all should have listened to you. You were trying to tell us something, but we—me, especially—thought you were being typically Risa."

"And typically Risa is…" Risa started.

"A stubborn, strong, caring, *good* person," Aria finished, "even if I haven't told you." She waved off Risa's reply, and Risa suspected it was because her sister saw the tears she fought to contain. "Who knows about this?"

"Josh and Eliana. And Ry."

"How did Josh take it?"

Risa put her hand to her head. "Not well. He's furious at me for not telling him about his son."

"I have another grandson, then," Joseph said, glancing from Risa to where Mateo, snuggled in his quilt, slumbered on, oblivious to the adults around him.

"He's not my son or your grandchild," Risa said, and it qualified as among the most painful words she'd ever forced herself to say. "He never really was."

Thankfully Aria changed the subject—only to one Risa was even less ready to confront. "What about Ry? What does he say about all of this?"

"He was better than Josh, but I think whatever it was that we had between us might be over." She swallowed hard against a surge of bitter realization. "I abandoned my baby the same way his mother abandoned him. He can't get past that. I don't think he'll ever fully accept it, and I can't live with that."

"You don't know that for sure," Aria persisted. "Give him some time. Josh, too. Eliana will help him see things clearly."

Unconvinced, Risa shook her head. "Eliana is pregnant and just learned her husband fathered a child with another woman. I doubt she's seeing things too clearly. And if I don't know what clear is right now, how can Josh? Or Ry, for that matter?"

She didn't realize how despondent she sounded until Aria stood up and came over to wrap her in a tight hug. "Give yourself a break. This was so brave of you. I can't even imagine how hard this has been. All these years…"

Pride at first kept Risa from breaking down in front of Aria. But her sister refused to yield to her this time, and Risa's resistance crumbled. They held on to each other as true sisters, hearts open, all past competitiveness meaningless, sharing pain, forgiveness and hope.

"Something good has come of this, then," Joseph said, turning both his daughters toward him. "If that boy has brought you together after all this time, then he's a blessing. I can only hope he's with a family that agrees."

"Do you know what happened to him?" Aria asked, unconsciously echoing Ry's criticism of her never looking back, though Risa knew that wasn't her sister's meaning. "I'm sorry. If you don't want to talk about it—"

"It's not that," Risa said. "It's Ry's biggest issue with this—that I never found out what happened to my baby after I gave him up. He can't live with the idea that I might have left a child in the same circumstances as he grew up in." She took a deep breath. "I said I'd help Josh try to find him. I don't feel very good about it, but Josh is going to do it whether I'm with him or not. Both he and Ry agree it's something I should have done a long time ago."

"Ry Kincaid needs to butt out," Aria muttered. "Or have his kicked. This doesn't have anything to do with him."

Shaking his head at Aria, Joseph told Risa, "If you and Josh are going to do this, I can help. After all these years taking in foster children, I know people in several orphanages and adoption agencies. I'll pull in a few favors."

"You can count on me, too," Aria added. "I can also talk to Cort, if you want. He's got a year of law school left, but this is going to be his area of expertise, and he has a lot of connections with social services from when he worked with the sheriff's department. I'm sure he'd help."

"We'll figure this out, Risa." Joseph held out his arms, beckoning Risa into the comfort of his embrace. She went unhesitatingly, desperate for his forgiveness, his understanding. "I'm proud of you, honey, so very proud of you for telling Josh and us. But I've always been proud of you. You have so much to give, Risa, so much you do give. Don't ever think otherwise."

"We're family, you know," Aria said, coming over to put a kiss in her sister's hair. "You're not alone. You never were."

For the first time in her life, Risa allowed herself to believe it was true.

The day after Risa's revelations to Josh, Ry found himself standing in the great room at the big house confronted by Jed and Del and wondering why the hell he'd agreed to this.

Jed had called him that morning, soundly cursing Josh for getting Del all worked up again and demanding Ry bring Risa to the ranch. Ry had bluntly told Jed to stay out of it and away from Risa, and hung up.

He'd tried to call Risa to warn her, but she hadn't answered her cell, and both her father and the staffer at the shelter had said she wasn't there. Frustrated, unsettled and angry with the situation, he was debating whether to track Risa down in person when his cell barked again. It was Josh, asking if he'd meet him at the ranch.

"What's the point of me showing up?" he'd asked his brother. "If you're expecting me to drag Risa over there, you can forget it. There's no way I'd put her through that."

"Now you're her protector? You weren't takin' her side yesterday."

Guilt slapped him. "This conversation is over." He was a second from cutting the connection when Josh spoke up.

"Ry, wait." He could hear Josh's effort to bank his temper. "I'm sorry. That was outta line. Look, I know this is askin' a lot, but Dad wants Risa there, and since I know that's not happenin', you're the next best thing. She's told you more than she's told anyone. And I could use someone else to help me talk Dad out of whatever scheme he's got in mind."

Ry, still smarting from Josh's dig, almost refused, but then Josh played his trump card.

"If you don't show up, there won't be anybody there defendin' Risa. And since Mom just moved back in with Dad, I've got the feelin' she'll be needin' a friend."

She could, but Ry doubted if she wanted it to be him. Yet imagining the ways Jed and Del could and probably would crucify her behind her back, he couldn't say no to Josh.

Jed had started in the moment Ry and Josh walked in the door twenty minutes later. "Where is she?" A harsh cough accompanied the snapped-out question, and Del, hovering next to him, glared at Ry and Josh in turn.

"Now, honey, you know you're not supposed to be gettin' all upset," she told Jed, fussing with the pillow behind his back.

"Leave it," Jed grumbled. He fixed his scowl on Ry. "I asked you to bring the girl. I want to hear from her what proof she's got this boy is Josh's."

"She's lyin'," Del said sharply. "Why, everyone knows Risa Charez slept with practically every boy in town back then. And she's no better now. Look at the way she's been carryin' on with you." She tossed her chin at Ry.

Ry's temper flared, overriding caution. He took a step forward, ready to tell Del Garrett what she could do with her gossip about Risa.

Josh's grip on his shoulder held him back. "Let me handle this."

They stared at each other, a silent battle of wills. Then Ry shook off Josh's hand. "Do it, or I will."

"Risa's not lyin', Mom," Josh said. "Like it or not, the boy's mine."

"I just don't see how that can be true."

Jed snorted. "Then you're blind, woman. You should've seen this comin' a long ways back."

"Like father, like son, you mean?" Ry said.

"Watch your mouth, boy. This ain't about me."

"No, it's not." Del's voice raised an octave. "Josh was just a boy when that little hussy seduced him. He didn't know what he was doin'."

Josh rolled his eyes. "I knew exactly what I was doin', with Risa and all the rest before Ellie. I'm not proud of it, but believe me, none of 'em ever took advantage of me. If anything, it was the other way around."

"That's not true," Del sniffed. "She's the slut, and now she's tryin' to get something out of you with this wild story of hers—"

"One of you better get her out of here or shut her the hell up," Ry snarled, fed up with the lot of them.

Del gave a little squeak and stumbled back a step.

"You're not helpin', Mom," Josh muttered.

Appraising Ry with a hard stare, Jed then shook his head. "Looks like you got it bad for that girl."

Ry didn't bother denying it, because it would be a lie. Instead, he returned a stony silence, daring Jed to take it any further.

"What are you gonna do about this?" Jed turned to Josh.

"I told you, Risa and I are gonna find him. Then we'll decide what to do."

"What's there to decide? He's your boy. You got a right to know him."

"It's not that simple," Josh said. "If he's with good people—"

"It don't matter who he's with. He's family."

"It matters," Ry intervened. "But what doesn't make a damn bit of difference is what you think. This is Risa and Josh's business, not yours. So do yourself and the rest of us a favor and stay the hell out of it."

For a moment, Jed, despite being sick and recovering from his broken hip, looked like he wanted to throw a punch or at least the nearest bottle at him. Ry didn't flinch, and after a few seconds, Jed let out a laugh.

"You may not like it, boy, but you're more like me than any of the rest of 'em, guts, jackass stubbornness, devil's temper and all."

He didn't like it. But he couldn't change it, anymore than he could change the course of events he'd set in motion with his misplaced doubts and mistrust of Risa. She'd looked to him for forgiveness and acceptance, and he'd let her down.

Leaving the ranch, with nothing settled but Josh's resolve to find his son, Ry admitted Jed had been right— he had it bad.

Chapter Seventeen

Hiding was the coward's way out, but Risa had no intention of answering Jed Garrett's summons to Rancho Pintada or Ry's messages, since she suspected Jed had enlisted him to talk her into the meeting. She'd agreed to help Josh find their baby, but that didn't include subjecting herself to his father's browbeating or Del's accusations and name-calling.

She'd turned off her cell and stayed put at her father's house until late afternoon, when she judged the meeting would be over. Now, feeling she could breathe easier, at least for the rest of the day, she decided to head over to the shelter for a few hours.

Her plan to seek a few hours of relative peace and quiet there fell apart the minute she walked out the front door. A familiar SUV was stopped in the driveway, and Eliana Garrett was closing the driver's door.

"Eliana, hi, this is a surprise," she managed as Eliana stepped up to meet her at the door. *An unwelcome one,* she added silently, because she couldn't imagine Josh's wife had come for a friendly chat.

"I'm sure it is. May I come in for a minute?"

"Of course, you must be freezing." Bracing herself for an awkward conversation at best, Risa led Eliana into the living room, taking her coat from her.

She half expected to see censure, hurt or anger in the other woman's eyes. But Eliana smiled a little as she sat down on the couch with Risa and smoothed a hand over the small curve of her belly that was her growing child.

"Josh said you didn't show up at the ranch today," Eliana said.

"There wasn't any point. Nothing was going to get resolved. I'd apologize, but it would be a lie."

"I don't blame you. I'm glad you didn't go. From what Josh told me, the only thing that did get accomplished was Jed and Del making Ry mad." Eliana paused, then added softly, "Ry obviously cares a lot about you."

Deliberately ignoring Eliana's last observation, Risa struggled for the right words to say to her. "I don't know how to tell you how sorry I am about all of this. I never meant to hurt you."

"Risa, listen to me," Eliana said firmly. "I've done nothing but think about this since you and Ry told us. At first, it hit hard, really hard. I had all of these thoughts, visions, questions about you and Josh."

"I understand," Risa said quietly.

"But then," Eliana went on, "I realized how ridiculous I was being. It was so long ago. And if I were going to worry about every girl, every woman Josh slept with before we got together, well, I'd need some major Botox injections about now."

Risa's small smile quickly came and went. "It can't be easy, knowing. You were here in the same town, and people talk."

"It doesn't matter now, though, does it? His past is his past. Nothing more. It's part of what makes him who he is today. And I love that man, the whole package."

"I hope Josh knows how lucky he is. Not everyone would be as accepting and forgiving of the past as you."

"You're thinking of Ry, aren't you?"

"Yes, but that's not what's important right now." She couldn't focus on what might be left of her relationship with Ry when her confession could have cost Eliana and Josh so much more. "I half expected you'd hate me. There are a lot of women who would. The last thing I wanted was to mess up your marriage."

Eliana reached over and briefly squeezed Risa's hand. "I don't hate you. You were just a teenager, and you dealt with it the best you could at the time. Josh and I will weather this, don't worry. Like I said, I love him, and I know he loves me. And I'll love his child if it turns out we need to take action to get him back."

"I hope it doesn't come to that," Risa said.

"Me, too. But we won't know until we find him. And when we do, we'll deal with it together."

After spending her life feeling unworthy of and therefore avoiding the closeness and support other women seemed to take for granted from each other, it felt strange to Risa to suddenly be allied with Eliana, especially considering the circumstances. Strange, but a comfort, dispelling some of the loneliness she'd lived with for so long.

"Are you still coming to the wedding?" Eliana asked. "I know Duran and Lia are expecting you."

"No, not now."

Eliana looked troubled. "If it's because of this, I can tell you that nobody is going to be pointing fingers. It was a shock, but everybody in the family understands."

"Everybody?" Risa slanted a skeptical glance her way.

"Well, okay, everybody besides Jed and Del. But Ry isn't going to let either of them corner you or bring any of this up. Josh is determined this will stay within the family, and he's definitely got Ry's support on that."

"I appreciate that, but the only reason I was invited to the wedding was because I was going with Ry. We're not—" It hurt to think of what they weren't. Risa wasn't sure if they were even friends any more. It didn't stop her loving him, but she couldn't pretend to everyone that things were good between them, either. "Plus, I'm really busy. I'm giving a New Year's Eve party at the shelter. I thought it would be a celebration of new beginnings for the women there."

"It could be for you, too," Eliana said. "Ry cares about you, Risa. Everyone can see it."

"Maybe he does. But he's not as forgiving as you. He can't accept my giving up my baby, never finding out what happened to him and not telling Josh before now." Risa looked away, past the warmth of the familiar room and Eliana's sympathetic eyes, to the view outside the window, cold and blanketed in snow.

"If he can't forget the past," she said, "I don't see how we can have a future."

"It was a beautiful wedding, wasn't it?"

Lost in thought, Ry didn't hear Maya come up behind

him until he felt a light tap on his shoulder. He gave a slight start, turning to find Sawyer's beautiful red-haired wife studying him.

"I came over to wish you a happy New Year's Eve, but I think I'm wasting my breath," she said lightly. "You look like you're somewhere else."

"No, just taking a break from all the noise. Parties aren't my thing." From his isolated spot in a small sitting area outside the main ballroom of the elegant Santa Fe hotel, he glanced back at the festive crowd gathered to celebrate Duran and Lia's marriage. "It seems like a strange day for a wedding."

Maya took a sip from her champagne glass. "It depends on your perspective. It's a great night for new beginnings."

Every time he was around this woman she seemed to talk double-talk. He always had the feeling she knew more about people than they knew about themselves. Including him. "You trying to tell me something?"

"Where's Risa?"

"So you can be straightforward."

"Much to my family's annoyance at times," she said with a smile.

"She's having a party at the shelter."

"So, you've done your family duty here. Your brother and his new wife had a gorgeous ceremony. You've had your glass of champagne and piece of cake. Why aren't you where you need to be?"

Ry's first instinct was to tell Maya it wasn't her business, that he didn't need her advice when it came to Risa. But there was something in her eyes—a sympathetic understanding—that breached his already shaken defenses. "Because she doesn't need me there."

"You're so sure of that?"

"Yeah, I am. I messed things up over this whole thing with the baby. I don't know if we can fix it."

"Do you want to?" Maya asked.

He focused on a distant point, his memories of Risa so strong he could almost feel her beside him. He missed her, the strength of it an ache in his chest that nothing relieved.

Maya waited a lingering moment then said, "Ry?"

Looking back, he met her eyes. "Yeah?"

"Get out of here."

Ry unlocked the deadbolt on the front door of the shelter, the noise from the kids, music, games and general havoc greeting him inside. He made his way through the group of women and their carefully selected friends and family, greeting the kids and moms with a special hug for Gustavo as he plucked him off the floor and spun him around.

"Happy New Year, Ry!" Gustavo belted out the greeting then blew his noisemaker in Ry's face.

Paper plates, cups, napkins and toys littered the den, and Ry wished he'd been there the whole night with Risa and the rest of them. "Hey, guy, where's Risa?"

Gustavo pointed to the kitchen, and Ry set him back on the floor. With a parting grin, the little boy ran off to join a group of kids, leaving Ry to make his way through the throng to the kitchen.

He found Risa at the sink, washing dishes side by side with Dolores. It took a major effort of will not to pull her into his arms and kiss her until they both didn't care about anything else but loving each other. The uncertainty of his welcome stopped him. The holidays had come and gone without them seeing each other; she'd backed out of going to the wedding with him and hadn't invited him here tonight. He didn't have a clue where things stood between them, or if there was even a *them* left.

"I thought that was you," she said, turning, her face revealing nothing of her feelings.

"What gave me away?"

"Gustavo. I'm pretty sure the neighbors know you're here, too." She looked him up and down. "Although that suit is a good disguise. You look good, Ry," she added. Her voice was softer, and he imagined there was a note of longing in it.

"You, too. Better than good." He took his time to appraise her, from the kicky red headband in her hair to the clingy little red dress and shiny silver high heels. "Wow."

He got himself a smile for that, small but enough to go straight to his head. "I'll take that," she said.

"You shouldn't be doing dishes in that getup."

She shrugged. "I gave the staff the night off."

"You two go," Dolores urged. "We're fine. We're all friends and family here."

"I have nowhere to go," Risa said lightly.

"How about a walk?" he suggested. "It just started snowing. Shouldn't be too slick, yet."

Her hands buried in suds, Dolores bumped Risa with her elbow. "Go. Take a break. You work too much. *No bueno*. Makes you boring."

"Well, I've never been told that before," Risa returned with a laugh that sounded forced.

She locked gazes with Ry, and for the first time in his life he worried that he might be reduced to begging if she said no. He'd told Maya he didn't know if he could fix things with Risa, but he had to try.

Finally, she nodded. "I'll get my coat and boots."

New snow settled under their boots as they walked side by side along a path behind the shelter. Ice-white flakes glistened in their hair, reflecting soft light beneath the full moon.

The beauty of the winter night was lost on Risa. Despite his proximity, she kept her distance from Ry, avoiding his reach for her hand. Though she hadn't seen him in weeks, she still felt raw, vulnerable with him, the hurt at their last parting as new as if it were yesterday.

She was surprised and confused by his arrival tonight. He had to have left his brother's wedding reception early, making the drive from Santa Fe to her doorstep—why?

She wanted to ask, but the question came out differently. "How was the wedding?"

"Nice."

Smiling, she shook her head, drawing his gaze.

"What's so funny?" he asked.

"You and your one-word descriptions. I'm sure it was very romantic and elegant. Aria told me all about their plans."

"Guess it was." He shoved his hands in his pockets, staring out in front of them. "How was your party?"

"Crazy. I think everyone had fun."

"I got that."

Another long silence fell between them, and then Ry abruptly stopped, taking her hand in his before she could deny him. "I wanted to be with you. These last weeks... They've been hell."

"Ry—"

"I know I hurt you. I'm trying to figure this out. But I can't do it if you aren't with me."

"How can I be? This situation with the baby—you aren't going to figure it out until Josh and I find him, and even then, that might not be enough for you. If we find out he's not happy, you'll never be able to accept it. You'll never be able to accept me," she finished miserably. Tugging her hand free from his, she took a step from him. "I can't stay with you and know that. I—" *love you, need you* "—care too much about you."

"And you don't think I care enough about you to let it go?"

"I don't know, Ry. Can you?"

She desperately wanted him to say yes, for him to take her in his arms and tell her none of it mattered, that he loved her for who she was, past be damned.

Jerking around, he raked his hands through his hair, then spun back to her. "I want to. I need time."

Her heart broke, but she wouldn't let him see it. "Take time then," she said quietly. "I just can't be there while you make up your mind."

She left him standing there alone and hurried back to the shelter with tears icy on her face and the knowledge she'd lost him darker and more bitterly chill than the midnight cold.

Chapter Eighteen

They had arranged the meeting at a sledding spot outside Santa Fe because there were going to be no formal introductions, just a casual encounter, as if Risa and Josh were simply another couple enjoying the late winter sunshine. The boy's parents had been wary, protective, reluctantly agreeing after Risa and Josh explained their reasons for wanting to see their son. However, the parents had refused to allow Eliana and Ry to come along.

Families congregated at the biggest slope to sled down the hill, and Risa and Josh stopped to watch them. It only took Risa a few minutes to find him. She lightly gripped Josh's arm, and he followed her gaze to a short distance away where a couple and their two sons were dragging sleds up to the top of the hill.

The man noticed them standing there and, after gesturing in their direction with a quick word to his wife, walked over. "You found us," he said. He glanced at his family. "Shane's the older one. We adopted Cody a few years later." Pausing, the man appraised Josh. "Shane looks like you."

Josh, studying the boy, said quietly, "I wondered."

"This is difficult," the man said slowly. "My wife and I understand your reasons for wanting to see him. But we love both our boys. Shane's a good kid, and he's happy. We need to know—"

"We're not staying," Risa spoke up. She looked at Josh, and after the smallest of hesitations, he nodded. "We just needed to know, too."

"And now that we do, we're goin' home." Josh offered a hand to the other man, who grasped it firmly. "Thanks. You've got yourself a great family."

The man smiled. "I think so." He turned as a shriek of laughter heralded the start of a snowball fight between his sons. "I'd better get back."

Risa allowed herself one last, lingering look at the boy who, ever so briefly, had been her son, too. Her vision blurred, dazzled by the glistening white and the sunlight, and with a small smile, she turned and left part of her past behind, playing in the new snow.

Hauling the last of his ice ski gear inside after a day trip with a client, Ry was shaking off the snow and the cold when the sound of a vehicle pulling up to the cabin froze him midgesture in hanging up his duster. The small spark of hope it could be Risa irritated him. He hadn't talked to her since New Year's Eve. She'd shut him out, and he was angry at himself for caring.

He'd told himself it didn't matter. All these years, his

chosen solitude had protected him from disappointment and heartache. He could go back to that life and forget that he'd allowed himself to become dependent on her for his happiness, convince himself the ache in his chest wasn't permanent.

But when he opened the door to Duran and the hope it was Risa died, he knew he was lying to himself. He could never go back.

"You haven't answered your phone in almost two weeks," his brother said by way of greeting. "I thought I'd try you here."

"I just got back from doing a couple of jobs in Utah. Cell service there doesn't exist." They moved into the living room, and Ry nudged Bear aside so he could get a fire started. "What's going on?" he asked Duran over his shoulder.

"Josh and Risa are coming home this afternoon."

Ry lost his grip on the log he was adding to the pile in the fireplace, and it hit with a clatter at his feet. He picked it back up and carefully laid it on the stack. "Didn't know they were gone."

"Josh said he told you they found the boy's family." At Ry's nod, Duran went on. "He and Risa went to Santa Fe a couple of days ago to arrange a meeting. I thought Risa might have said something."

"Haven't seen her," Ry said shortly. After lighting the fire, he got to his feet and reluctantly faced Duran.

"Is that because you don't want to?"

"Is this what you wanted to see me about? Because if you came here for true confessions, I'm fresh out."

"I came here because I thought you might need a friend—or a brother. You've been pretty miserable since the holidays, and I'm guessing a lot of it has to do with whatever's going on between you and Risa. I know you're in love with her—"

"No. I'm not." But Ry couldn't look his brother in the eyes.

"Am I supposed to believe that?" Duran gave Ry a few seconds of silence. "What happened?"

"What happened was I screwed up and she left me." Ry forced the words out. He wasn't good at spilling his guts so someone else could analyze them, but the weeks without Risa had been the worst and the loneliest of his life. Maybe talking to Duran would help combat the feeling he'd lost the best part of himself when he lost her. "I was the first person she told about the baby. She trusted me because I said I didn't give a damn about what she'd done in the past."

"But this was different," Duran said, "because of your past."

"All I could think was what if that kid ended up like me? I made it about me, when I should have been there for her. And then, when she left, I blamed her for making me—" He came to a full stop.

"Care?"

Ry rubbed a hand over his face. "Yeah. I've avoided it all this time. Now I see why."

"I hate to break it to you, but it's too late to take it back. You're going to have to learn to live with it."

"Easy for you to say. At least you've had some experience."

"There's only one way to get that. Talk to Risa. Tell her how you feel."

"And then?"

Duran smiled a little. "And then tell her that you love her."

* * *

A short distance from where he'd left his truck parked, Josh surprised Risa by stopping at one of the benches and brushing away the snow so they could sit down.

"We can't go back," she said, thinking he was having second thoughts about leaving their child behind without becoming a part of his life.

"I don't want to. It wouldn't be right, for any of us. But I wanna say I'm sorry for blamin' all of this on you. You did the best thing for him. I wouldn't have been there for you. In fact, back then," he said with a rueful grimace, "I'm pretty sure I would have hightailed it as far away from you as I could get."

"We both made mistakes."

"Yeah, but I haven't been payin' for 'em all these years like you." Putting an arm around her shoulders, Josh drew her into a hug. "Let it go, Risa. Forgive yourself."

She held him, accepting the comfort of a friend, and felt a change inside her, a lessening of the weight of the guilt she'd carried. In its wake came something she hadn't known for a long time: a sense of peace.

On the way back to the truck, searching his pocket for his keys, Josh asked, "So, are you gonna call Ry and let him know we're on the way home?"

"No. Unless you told him, he doesn't know we're here," Risa answered flatly. "And if that's your way of asking how things are going between us, they aren't and haven't been for a while."

"I'm thinkin' part of that's my fault."

"We were having trouble before I told you about this. His past and mine kept coming between us."

Josh started the truck but made no move to put it in

gear. "Maybe once he knows what happened here, he'll come around."

"Maybe, but I don't know if it's worth waiting to find out." She stared out in front of them for a moment, then burst out, "I'm mad at him. I understand where he's coming from, but I didn't deserve him telling me he didn't care about my past and then changing his mind because he couldn't separate it from his."

"Nope, you're right. You're wastin' your time on him. Everybody's been warnin' you he wasn't any better than the old man. Too bad you love each other."

Risa glared at him, annoyed by his broad grin. "He's not in love with me."

"I notice you didn't deny bein' in love with him," Josh said smugly, as if he'd scored a victory over her. "And yeah, he is. He just doesn't like it."

That was probably true. Ry didn't know anything about being loved and loving, and being faced with feelings he couldn't explain or control would kick in all his defenses. He'd hurt her and she'd left him, and that had prompted his own retreat.

What was certainly true was she loved him. It seemed all her life she'd wanted love and acceptance, but never expected it. Yet she'd found it in the most unlikely man. Ry had refused to accept her insecurities, taught her to have faith in herself and to believe she was worthy of being loved and loving in return.

Now she had to make a choice: to give up or fight for their love.

"You ready to go home?" Josh asked.

"Yes," she said and found herself smiling. "Yes, I am."

And this time she meant it.

* * *

Ry debated calling her, threw out that choice on the idea it would be harder for her to tell him to go to hell in person, and decided instead to wait for her at her dad's house.

Joseph hadn't questioned his showing up unannounced or his intention to be there when Risa got home. The older man had shown him to a seat in the living room, then disappeared almost immediately, saying he had to finish the few chores he'd started before Ry's arrival.

Ry restlessly paced the room, turning over in his mind what he wanted to say to her and how he was going to say it, until he heard Josh's truck pull into the driveway, doors being slammed shut and voices approaching the house.

"Hey, we didn't know you'd be here," Josh said, dropping Risa's bag in the entryway.

"Yeah, guess not." Ry answered his brother, but his eyes locked with Risa's and Josh might not have been there.

"Well, I gotta go. Ellie's waitin' on me. Don't be a stranger," Josh told Risa, and Ry noticed how easily she smiled and hugged him.

"I won't, promise," she said.

"That goes for you, too, Ry." And with a wink and a grin for Risa, Josh was out the door, leaving them alone.

They stood there looking at each other until Risa finally broke the silence. "I didn't expect you here."

"I didn't expect me here, either. I wanted—I needed to see you."

Risa searched his eyes for a moment then started stripping off her coat. "The trip went well," she said, walking past him into the living room. "We got to see my little boy, and he's fine. He's with people who love him, and he's happy. Josh and I agreed that he's better off not knowing anything about us."

"Good, but I didn't come here to talk about that."

"I thought you'd want to know. It mattered to you before."

To hell with talking. Ry strode over, grasped her shoulders, pulled her to him and kissed her long and deep. "That's what matters," he said huskily. "You deserve better than me, but I can't let you go."

"I deserve a man who loves me, like I love him." She laid her palm against his cheek, and he could see in her eyes all the love and tenderness he'd sworn he could live without offered to him if he was willing to give it in return.

"I love you, Risa," he said, and though the words were unfamiliar coming from him, nothing had ever sounded or felt so right. "I'm sorry. I know I hurt you—"

Her fingers touched his lips, stopping him. "I love you. I always will."

"I don't care what's past anymore," he said, not willing to let this go until he convinced her he'd chosen her over holding on to memories of a life that had shaped him but no longer owned him. "Whatever happened before, I want us to be together now. You saved me. I can't think about being without you."

There were tears in her eyes, and yet she smiled. "I think we saved each other," she said softly. Putting her arms around him, she drew him into a kiss that was more promise than passion, more forgiveness than desire, and all loving.

"Come home with me," Ry murmured against her mouth.

"Is it home?"

"It will be, if you're there."

"I'll need some clothes." She lightly kissed the hollow of his throat.

"Doubt it."

"And my toothbrush."

"You can borrow mine."

"Toothbrush sharing is a pretty big commitment," she lightly teased. "Are you sure you're ready for it?"

Ry wrapped her even closer, and suddenly it wasn't teasing. "I'm ready," he promised. "I mean it, Risa. This is permanent."

"For me, too. Of course—" she smiled again "—you know what people are going to say when they find out we're living together."

"That I love my wife?" She stared, and he laced her hands with his, kissed her and said, "Say yes."

"Yes." And then she was laughing and kissing him as he lifted her off her feet, holding her with no intention of ever letting her go.

With her answer, the last remnants of the past faded away, leaving Ry with only a clear, bright path to a future with Risa and, for the first time, love.

Epilogue

Five years later

Sunlight filtered through the trees, dappling the grasses with gold, warming the breeze and the shadows of Jed Garrett's final resting place. They'd buried him, as he'd wanted, on a far corner of Rancho Pintada, the site secluded, rarely visited except by stray bison or an occasional lone rider.

Ry thought the setting and the service—short, with only family in attendance—was a fitting epitaph for Jed. Jed had never been a real father to any of his sons, but in his own way, he'd brought them all together and given them the chance to become a true family.

It was a chance he'd once thought he'd never have and didn't want. But looking at Risa and then at the gathering of his brothers, their wives and children, he knew he'd gotten more than he'd ever imagined, and that this, at last, was home.

"Jed left quite the legacy," Risa commented as they walked hand in hand to the Jeep for the drive back to the big house.

"You mean the ranch?"

She smiled a little. "There's that, I suppose. But I meant the seven of you. I think his sons were his redemption."

He carried that thought with him into the crowded great room of the house, he and Risa making their way to where Duran and Lia were nudging Noah and three-year-old Faith toward the buffet table.

"Guess this is Del's last time playing hostess," Ry said, nodding in his stepmother's direction. Del, in expensive black, her poodle clutched in her arm, sat in Jed's favorite chair in the center of the great room, flanked by her sister and her aunt.

"I don't think she liked the idea of sharing the house," Duran said. "She's apparently going back to Taos with her sister in a few weeks."

Surprisingly to all of them, Jed had willed the ranch house and half ownership in the ranch itself to Rafe, going back on his long-held decision to split the ranch between his sons. Rafe had typically balked, but the rest of them had agreed that of all of them, it had been Rafe who'd put his heart and soul into Rancho Pintada and who most deserved to inherit the majority of it.

Rafe and Jule had offered Del a home at the ranch for as long as she wanted. But she'd refused, saying she preferred living with her recently widowed sister, where she'd still be close enough for frequent visits to Josh and Eliana and Tyler, their rambunctious four-year-old.

"It looks like the next big event in this family is going

NICOLE FOSTER   211

to be a wedding," Risa said. The others followed her gaze to where Cort and Laurel's oldest son, Tommy, recently turned eighteen, stood with his arm around Anna Tamar, his childhood sweetheart.

"Don't say that too loudly around Laurel," Cort said, overhearing Risa as he was on his way past to help Quin, the baby of his house, find a seat for lunch. "She's already having separation anxiety over Tommy moving out." Tommy was going to take over Rafe's smaller house on the ranch, and Rafe and Josh were grooming him to one day fill the role of foreman. "She knows it's gonna happen," Cort added, "but she'd like Tommy and Anna to give her a few years to get used to the idea of her little boy all grown up."

Anna wasn't the only one of Eliana's siblings being drawn into the Garrett family fold. Ry had become sole owner of his thriving business after Grady decided to retire a year back. He now had three guides working for him and had recently hired Eliana's oldest brother, Teo, taking him under his wing after Teo had asked for a job and a chance to learn the work.

Ry reluctantly separated from his wife as Aria came over to ask her sister's help in getting the rest of the kids settled.

"You still act like a newlywed," Sawyer teased, coming over to hand Ry a drink. "You never take your eyes off her."

"I noticed it hasn't stopped you, after what—ten years?" Ry countered. Even after a decade of marriage and three children, Ry knew Sawyer felt the same about Maya as Ry did about Risa. The years of shared joys and sorrows, trials and triumphs had only strengthened their love for one another, as it had for all of them.

It was late in the afternoon before Ry and Risa finally made it back home to their mountain sanctuary. They were sitting on the front porch of the cabin, Bear stretched out in the summer sun beside them, when Risa shifted to face him. "I have something to tell you."

"Okay," he said slowly, not sure what to make of her expression, mixed expectancy, barely concealed excitement, a hint of uncertainty.

"I've known for a few days now, but I wanted to wait until after this morning." Taking his hand, she pressed his palm against her stomach. "You're going to be a father."

Ry could only look at her, hit by a wash of intense happiness that left him speechless. Very gently, keeping his hand in place, he kissed her. Then, looking into her eyes he said huskily, "I love you."

"You're happy?"

"You have to ask?"

"I wasn't sure." She smiled, touched his face. "There was a time when you didn't want anything to do with family."

"That was before you."

"I changed your mind?" she asked, and there was wonder in her voice.

"No," he said, gathering her into his arms, holding her close and imagining the child they'd created with their love. "You changed my heart."

* * * * *

*Celebrate Harlequin's 60th anniversary with
Harlequin® Superromance®
and the DIAMOND LEGACY miniseries!*

*Follow the stories of four cousins as they come
to terms with the complications of love
and what it means to be a family.
Discover with them the sixty-year-old secret
that rocks not one but two families in...
A DAUGHTER'S TRUST
by Tara Taylor Quinn.*

*Available in September 2009 from
Harlequin® Superromance®*

RICK'S APPOINTMENT with his attorney early Wednesday morning went only moderately better than his meeting with social services the day before. The prognosis wasn't great—but at least his attorney was going to file a motion for DNA testing. Just so Rick could petition to see the child…his sister's baby. The sister he didn't know he had until it was too late.

The rest of what his attorney said had been downhill from there.

Cell phone in hand before he'd even reached his Nitro, Rick punched in the speed dial number he'd programmed the day before.

Maybe foster parent Sue Bookman hadn't received his message. Or had lost his number. Maybe she didn't want to talk to him. At this point he didn't much care what she wanted.

"Hello?" She answered before the first ring was complete. And sounded breathless.

Young and breathless.

"Ms. Bookman?"

"Yes. This is Rick Kraynick, right?"

"Yes, ma'am."

"I recognized your number on caller ID," she said, her voice uneven, as though she was still engaged in whatever physical activity had her so breathless to begin with. "I'm sorry I didn't get back to you. I've been a little…distracted."

The words came in more disjointed spurts. Was she jogging?

"No problem," he said, when, in fact, he'd spent the better part of the night before watching his phone. And fretting. "Did I get you at a bad time?"

"No worse than usual," she said, adding, "Better than some. So, how can I help?"

God, if only this could be so easy. He'd ask. She'd help. And life could go well. At least for one little person in his family.

It would be a first.

"Mr. Kraynick?"

"Yes. Sorry. I was…are you sure there isn't a better time to call?"

"I'm bouncing a baby, Mr. Kraynick. It's what I do."

"Is it Carrie?" he asked quickly, his pulse racing.

"How do you know Carrie?" She sounded defensive, which wouldn't do him any good.

"I'm her uncle," he explained, "her mother's—Christy's—older brother, and I know you have her."

"I can neither confirm nor deny your allegations,

Mr. Kraynick. Please call social services." She rattled off the number.

"Wait!" he said, unable to hide his urgency. "Please," he said more calmly. "Just hear me out."

"How did you find me?"

"A friend of Christy's."

"I'm sorry I can't help you, Mr. Kraynick," she said softly. "This conversation is over."

"I grew up in foster care," he said, as though that gave him some special privilege. Some insider's edge.

"Then you know you shouldn't be calling me at all."

"Yes… But Carrie is my niece," he said. "I need to see her. To know that she's okay."

"You'll have to go through social services to arrange that."

"I'm sure you know it's not as easy as it sounds. I'm a single man with no real ties and I've no intention of petitioning for custody. They aren't real eager to give me the time of day. I never even knew Carrie's mother. For all intents and purposes, our mother didn't raise either one of us. All I have going for me is half a set of genes. My lawyer's on it, but it could be weeks— months—before this is sorted out. Carrie could be adopted by then. Which would be fine, great for her, but then I'd have lost my chance. I don't want to take her. I won't hurt her. I just have to see her."

"I'm sorry, Mr. Kraynick, but…"

* * * * *

*Find out if Rick Kraynick will ever have
a chance to meet his niece.
Look for A DAUGHTER'S TRUST by
Tara Taylor Quinn,
available in September 2009.*